SPY FORCE

Don't miss any of the
SPY FORCE
missions!

SPY FORCE

mission:
Hollywood

BY DEBORAH ABELA · ILLUSTRATED BY GEORGE O'CONNOR

Aladdin Paperbacks
New York • London • Toronto • Sydney

ALADDIN PAPERBACKS
An imprint of Simon & Schuster Children's Publishing Division
1230 Avenue of the Americas, New York, NY 10020
Text copyright © 2003 by Deborah Abela
Illustrations copyright © 2006 by George O'Connor
All rights reserved, including the right of reproduction in whole or in part in any form.
ALADDIN PAPERBACKS and related logo are registered trademarks
of Simon & Schuster, Inc.
First published in Australia in 2003 by Random House Australia Pty Ltd
Published by arrangement with Random House Australia Pty Ltd
Also available in a Books for Young Readers hardcover edition.
Designed by Lucy Ruth Cummins
The text of this book was set in Goudy.
Manufactured in the United States of America
First Aladdin Paperbacks edition July 2007
10 9 8 7 6 5 4 3 2 1
The Library of Congress has cataloged the hardcover edition as follows:
Abela, Deborah, 1966-
Mission—Hollywood / Deborah Abela.
p.   cm.
Summary: Eleven-year-old Max and other Spy Force agents investigate a dark plot involving the movie industry as Max, Linden, and an unexpected guest work as extras on her father's latest film.
[1.Spies—Fiction. 2. Motion pictures—Production and direction—Fiction.
3. Friendship—Fiction. 4. Fathers and daughters—Fiction. 5. Space and time—Fiction.]
PZ7.A15937   Mirs 2006
[Fic]—22
2005051610
ISBN-13: 978-0-689-87360-7 (hc.)
ISBN-10: 0-689-87360-3 (hc.)
ISBN-13: 978-1-4169-3969-6 (pbk.)
ISBN-10: 1-4169-3969-5 (pbk.)

For Brian and
Shirley Decker

A TOP-SECRET LETTER FROM **MAX REMY**, WORLD-FAMOUS
SUPERSPY

Actually, I'm not that famous, but I should be after what
happened during our last mission. Linden and I had to do spy
training at a secret training facility in New York. And guess what?
Alex Crane, only the most brilliant spy in the world, was our
trainer. There were virtual cascades, simulated earthquake
chambers, and fights with deadly intruder robots. At first
I was pretty clumsy at it ... but after a while I got the
hang of it ... sort of.

Then Spy Force contacted us through our new palm
computers and asked us to be part of a mission! The
Annual Spy Awards night happens once a year, and the
best spies from all over the world are invited. This year
it was to be held on a secret island deep within a
medieval fortress, but that slimeball Mr. Blue intercepted
Spy Force intelligence and found out where it was
going to be. He arranged to bring the island's dormant
volcano to life, which left me and Linden only hours to
save the spy agencies of the world from a terrible,
explosive demise! Not only that—he also created a
Nightmare Vortex, this creepy device where we were
forced to face our darkest fears. Oh, and did I say
that Ella was there as well? Some help she was! At
one point I had to save her. What does Linden see
in her?

Anyway, I'd better go. Spy Force may call at any
moment and ask me to help them save the world.

Signing off from SECRET AGENT Max Remy,
SUPERSPY

CHAPTER 1

A Race with
Death and a
Moment of Terror

Chronicles of Spy Force:

The steep, snow-wrapped mountain plunged before her like a giant slide to white oblivion. A violent blizzard filled the skies and the risk of death was as real as the knife-edged cold filling the air. As Max Remy catapulted on her skis through this frozen wilderness, a crushing wind tore at the forest that swayed and lurched on either side of her. Then, in all this whitened chaos, Max was dealt her first blow.

A helicopter rose from the heart of the forest, its rotor blades creating an icy sprawl that left her momentarily blinded. One wrong move at this speed and Max knew she faced certain and instant death.

She raced through the storm, maintaining her balance, with the helicopter expertly following her every move as she navigated her way around protruding rocks as dangerous as land mines. She'd been on far more dangerous missions than this, and some chopper pilot on a thrill ride wasn't going to stop her now.

That is, until she came to Devil's Run.

Devil's Run was a slice of the mountain that fingered into a narrow ledge overlooking a jagged, rock-filled chasm. If she went over the edge, search parties wouldn't be sent out. Bodies that fell into Devil's Run were never found.

She tried to ski away from the edge just as a rabbit hopped in front of her. In an instant she swerved, avoiding the furry animal and earning herself a place on the powdery edge of the cliff. The hungry mouth of the chasm opened up below her. She fought against the image of death that filled her mind, and regained her composure as the chopper moved into position for a final swoop.

"So, that's how you want to play," Max muttered through clenched teeth.

Now the pilot would make his move. If he'd come to kill her, it would not take long.

Flurries of snow swept up from the chasm in waves, wanting to drag Max into its depths. She tried to pull away from the edge, but the helicopter forced her even closer.

Then her fate took a fiendish turn. A man sitting next to the pilot pulled out a Stun Blaster and aimed it straight at her.

Max glimpsed the immobilizing device and knew there was little chance of evading its life-sucking punishment. Her skis sent clumps of snow over the cliff beside her. If she didn't think fast, she'd soon follow. Then she had it. A cunning plan that would end her enemy's menacing flight. A foolproof idea that

"Max! Let me in."

Max jumped in her seat, her fingers plunging across the keyboard. She stared at the screen of her computer as snow billowed from Devil's Run, where she'd just fallen to her death. Why did her mother instinctively know the worst times to interrupt her? It was as if she had some kind of Max anti-fun radar.

"Phone for you, sweetie. And why do you always lock this door?"

It was purely for health reasons. If her mother had unrestricted access to her room, Max stood a good chance of her brain exploding. She turned back to the computer.

"Gotta go, Linden. I've got my own forces of evil to deal with."

Linden's face appeared in the corner of Max's screen, beaming in from his home in Mindawarra. "Too bad." He smiled victoriously. "Who'd have thought after all that, you'd end up as a permanent ice block?"

"You were about to be trounced by my great comeback plan. That is, until the abominable snow woman knocked on my door. See you on the weekend."

"Yeah. We'll see if those landings of yours have finally been sorted out," Linden said, smirking.

Max had this unfortunate knack for messy landings whenever she used the Time and Space Machine. She'd landed in garbage compactors, pig troughs, compost bins, and freshly laid cat poop. Ben and Francis had promised they'd fix the problem, and this weekend she was going back to Mindawarra to try it out.

"See ya then," Max said coolly, but in reality she missed the farm and couldn't wait to go back.

3

She shut down the Spy Force Ski Run game that they'd been playing. There were lots of great things about being part of Spy Force, and access to virtual spy missions on their computers was definitely one of them. The games weren't as good as the simulation chambers in the Spy Force Training Centers, but they were still a great way to help Max forget she shared her regular life with the Fun Terminator.

"Quickly now."

Max followed her mother to the hall, and as Max picked up the phone, she noticed her mother hovering nearby, displaying a bad case of looking obvious while trying to listen in. Max took the phone to the living room and closed the door.

"Hello?"

"So, how about it? Are you in?" Max's dad spoke to his daughter from the other side of the world.

There was a pause as the scowl on Max's face was replaced with an enormous grin. "I . . . that'd be . . . um . . . ," she stammered.

"Is that a yes?" Her dad lived in Hollywood with his new wife and had just asked her to visit.

"Yes!" Max finally managed. She was finding it hard to speak, when all she really wanted to do was run into the middle of the street and yell, "My dad wants me to visit him! Finally!"

"I've been trying to come out since last Christmas, but every time it seems possible, I get more work, so I thought the best solution was for you to come here."

Max felt so light with happiness, it was as if she were floating around the room. Until she remembered a small problem and came crashing down.

"Have you asked Mom?"

"Not yet. I wanted to speak with you first."

"Oh." Suddenly Max's rose-colored world became murky gray.

"Don't worry, Max. Leave everything to me."

She wanted to believe him, but after eleven years of sharing the same piece of loony land with her mother, she knew she was going to be hard to convince.

"Put your mom on and we'll sign off on this deal."

Max said good-bye and trudged to the living room door. When she pulled it open, she faced the giant ear of her mother.

"I was listening for termites, sweetie." Her mother fixed her hair in an attempt not to look awkward, which made her look even more awkward. "Does your father want to talk to me?" she asked in a girlie voice.

Max handed over the phone while trying to find even a slight resemblance between herself and the woman people said was her mother.

Her mother's voice danced across the tiles and marble surfaces of the kitchen. Whenever she spoke to Max's dad, she put on her Everything's Perfect voice. Max went to the living room to wait for the verdict.

After what felt like hours, Max heard her mother say good-bye. She raced to the kitchen to find her mother humming and preparing dinner. Something wasn't right. She never hummed, and usually after long conversations with Max's dad, she walked around clanging everything and wore a face that had just sucked a lemon. This time her mother was happy, and any time that happened, it usually meant bad news for Max.

"Everything all right, Mom?" she asked cautiously.

"Everything all right?" her mom replied.

"Yeah. You seem a little strange." Max watched as her mother polished a tomato so hard she was in danger of wearing it out.

"A little strange?"

"Yeah, is everything all right?"

"Of course everything's all right."

Now Max was really worried. "Could you stop repeating everything I say?"

"I'm not repeating everything you . . . sorry. Everything's fine."

This was how life was with her mother. Max felt as if she were on a stretching rack and her mother were enjoying every second of torturing her.

Just then the doorbell rang.

"Oh." Her mother walked toward the front door. "And Aidan will be joining us."

What? Why did her mother never tell Max when she'd

invited people over? And when were they supposed to talk about what her dad had said? Max bit into a carrot as she prepared to face another painful evening with her mother and her mother's try-hard boyfriend.

Over dinner the only sound accompanying the clinking of cutlery against plates was the sound of whales moaning on the stereo. Her mom found it relaxing. Max just wanted to scream. Eventually she couldn't take it any longer.

"Mom, I know what Dad asked you, and I'm almost twelve years old, and I don't think it's right that you treat me like a kid when I'm almost not a kid anymore, and anyway I can make up my own mind about what's good for me and—"

"Max," her mother interrupted in a caramelly sweet voice. "There's something I'd like to tell you." She looked across at Aidan, who was smiling like a kid about to meet Santa. "Aidan and I are getting married."

Wham! Max felt the ground quake beneath her, like Dorothy when her house was sucked up by the tornado on her way to Oz. Things were suddenly spinning out of control, and if they didn't stop soon, her stomach and everything in it was going to leap out of her mouth all over everyone. Her mother was talking so fast her lips were beginning to blur. Max heard none of it. It was as though someone had turned down the volume on her life, which had changed from barely tolerable into a twisting, tortuous nightmare.

She saw events unfold before her. Her mother would be wearing a hideous designer dress that would spill out from a gold-encrusted horse-drawn carriage. The church would be filled with stylish people she didn't know sitting listening to soppy reject eighties music while flowers bloomed out of the seats like an overgrown jungle. The wedding party, of which Max would be a member, would be dragged into a hairdressing salon to be tugged, pruned, and curled, only to come out looking like extras from a horror movie. And she'd be forced to wear a dress! She could see herself now, marching down the aisle puffed up like a chiffon-covered blimp.

She couldn't let it happen. She'd been patient with this Aidan business long enough, but as she took a deep breath to tell them exactly what she thought, a clump of alfalfa was sucked into her windpipe.

"Max?"

Even though Max couldn't breathe, it was a relief that her mother had finally stopped talking. Max's face became the color of an eggplant as air struggled to pass the grassy salad.

"Aidan! Quick, do something!"

Soon Max stopped being able to gasp at all. Then something weird happened. She felt as if she were floating, not like when she was on the phone floating, but really floating. She rose above her choking body as if it belonged to someone else. The horror of being Aidan's stepdaughter suddenly became someone else's problem, and she felt instantly calm, like those stories about people who have near-death experiences and float away from their bodies toward the light at the end of the tunnel.

But are then forcefully jerked back.

Max's eyes flung open as the shining teeth and bulging lips of Aidan came straight for her.

"Don't come any closer," Max wheezed at Aidan's reckless attempt at mouth-to-mouth resuscitation. She'd left the floating sensation and landed back in the doom of her mother's impending marriage.

She was lying on the floor, covered in alfalfa, sun-dried tomatoes, and seaweed.

"But what about Dad?"

"This has nothing to do with your dad," her mother said calmly, trying to pretend her only child hadn't nearly choked to death.

"Listen, sweetie . . ."

But Max didn't wait to hear the rest. She'd had enough for tonight and was heading as far away from the happy couple as possible.

She climbed the stairs to her room and locked the door against the whole idea, desperately wanting to turn back time so that her mother's news had never happened. As she lay on her bed clutching her pillow against her sore throat, she slowly saw the best day of her life turn into the worst. Max had one thought: From now on her life was as good as over.

CHAPTER 2

A Dangerous Discovery

After a night filled with dreams of headless horsemen steering out-of-control bridal carriages, and wedding cakes crammed with spiders, Max slumped through the next day at school with a heavy dose of sleep deprivation.

Toby Jennings saw her sitting by herself during recess and, not wanting to waste a perfect opportunity to rile her, got ready for a little entertainment.

"Sitting with all your friends, Max?" Sniggers rose behind him.

Usually this would be enough to get Max started on her own fiery comebacks, but instead she kept focusing on an ant crawling over her shoe. Not only that, after saying nothing, she got up and walked away.

Toby and his friends stared. It was the first time since Toby had met Max that she hadn't bitten back when he'd tried to provoke her.

Later, in class, he tried again.

"Max?" he leaned in and whispered. "There's an express delivery at the school office. That brain you ordered must finally be here."

Two Toby goons sitting in front of them splurted giggles into their chests.

Max stared at the math book she was doodling on and said nothing.

Toby gave it another shot. "Or maybe it's that money-back–guarantee personality you bought." He smiled, but Max kept on doodling as if she hadn't heard him.

Toby wasn't going to give up. "Or maybe it's that—"

"What?" Max looked up and noticed Toby had been talking to her.

"Max Remy, apparently what you have to say to Toby Jennings is infinitely more interesting than what we're talking about." Mr. Fayoud's eyebrows were zigzagging all over his face like the burning fuse on a stick of dynamite.

Toby smirked.

"No, Mr. Fayoud. Sorry," Max muttered.

And that was it. No blaming. No yelling. Nothing.

Toby was really worried now. If Max stopped reacting to his teasing, school wasn't going to be half as much fun. Something had to be done.

At lunchtime he followed her as she made her way to the far end of the playground. She sat on a bench beneath tall trees and took out her lunch box. Toby hid behind the trees and watched her closely.

Max bit into a Japanese sushi roll as her eyes darted around the playground, making sure she wasn't being watched. Then she picked up her bag and pulled out her palm computer.

"Hey!" exclaimed Toby to himself. "It's that gadget Max had when Linden was here at Hollingdale."

Max pressed a few keys and began speaking into it. Toby heard Linden's name and some hushed talk about a time and space machine. He remembered the machine from when he'd stolen Max's diary and read her spy stories out loud to the other kids. He also remembered Max and Linden laughing when he teased them about being spies. They laughed as if they knew something he didn't.*

"Maybe you *are* a superspy." As soon as Toby said it, he felt ridiculous. Why would anyone choose Max to be a superspy? She wasn't even chosen for any of the sports teams at school. But maybe, just maybe, it was true.

"At least it'd explain why you're so weird."

Toby strained to hear more, but Max closed the device and put it in her bag.

"Too bad, Max. I saw your little gadget." If Max was up to something exciting, Toby was going to find out about it. First, though, he needed to get his hands on the communication device she had in her bag—to discover more about the Time and Space Machine. As the bell chimed throughout the school and Toby watched Max make her way to class, the beginnings of a cunning plan ignited in his brain.

*See Mission: *Spy Force Revealed*.

CHAPTER 3

The Bride of
Frankenstein in
Mindawarra

After school Max walked out the gate to find her mother parked in the no parking zone, applying lipstick and eyeliner in the rearview mirror. A buildup of traffic struggled to make its way past the car as her mother remained oblivious of the fact that this was simply another of a million embarrassing things she did. Then she noticed Max and sounded the horn.

"Hurry up, sweetie! We're late already," she cried, waving a red scarf out the window.

Max walked past a line of kids blowing her kisses and calling each other "sweetie" as they waved hankies and pretended to apply invisible lipstick. She walked even faster to the car, wondering what it would be like to be an orphan.

Her mother gave her what had become in recent months her regular slobbery kiss before taking off at high speed and just missing the school bus that had to swerve to avoid her. Max sank into her seat as the driver slammed on the horn and the kids in the bus made faces at her.

Her mother prattled on about her day and the romantic weekend she and Aidan were about to go on. Max tried to erase all the disgusting thoughts that wormed into her mind. What is it about adults that they don't get that this stuff should happen in private?

She stared out the window. Her mother hadn't mentioned her dad's phone call or his invitation to come visit. She could at least tell her she'd said no, then Max could get on with how miserable her life was. Eventually, as the trees and farms of the country began to appear, her mother stopped talking and the silence began. Max felt her mother's eyes flick toward her, wanting, she knew, some kind of Hollywood mother–daughter bonding session that would make everything all right.

"Is something bothering you, sweetie?" Her mother asked like someone who hadn't been involved in Max's life over the last twenty-four hours.

"Have you told Dad about you and Aidan?" Max couldn't bring herself to say the word "marriage."

"Yes. He knows."

"Did he say anything else?"

"No." Then she remembered. "Oh, he did mention something about you going to visit, but I told him you and I had the wedding to organize."

Her mother's face inflated into a plump smile as Max's heart fell to her feet. She'd thought the answer would be no, but hearing it took away any hope of it not being true.

"I haven't seen Dad for ages." Max held back tears.

"I know," her mother said softly. Then she brightened again as if she had the answer to all their problems. "But you and I will be so busy. We can go shopping together, pick out material, decide on table settings. It'll be fun."

Unless someone had rewritten the definition of fun to mean "a hideous time where one is subjected to the tortures of one's mother," fun didn't have a vague chance of happening. "Yeah, fun," she repeated dully.

Max saw her mother's smile falter. She wanted her mom to be happy and would even get used to Aidan if she didn't have to spend too much time with him, but Max missed her dad and there was this feeling in her stomach only he could fix.

They drove on in thick silence.

At Ben and Eleanor's farm, Max didn't wait for her mother to turn off the engine before she grabbed her bag and ran toward Eleanor's outstretched arms.

"Now, that's what I call a proper hello!" Eleanor hugged her niece into the many folds of her clothes.

Max breathed in Eleanor's familiar smell, which was a mixture of baked dinners, grassy paddocks, and old-fashioned soap. She clung to her aunt and wished she could stay there forever, away from news of weddings, arguments, and the fact that she wasn't going to see her dad.

"That's enough for her. Now it's my turn."

Ben grabbed Max and swooped her into the air. She giggled as he swung her around his bulky frame before plonking her back on the ground. After Max regained her balance, she saw a tall man walking toward her from the shed.

"Now, here's someone who's been looking forward to seeing you," Ben whispered.

It was Francis, Ben's brother who'd come to live with them after Max and Linden brought him back from London.*

*For more exciting details see Mission: Spy Force Revealed.

21

"It's good to see you again," he muttered as he tried to figure out where to put his hands. Ben and Francis were total opposites. Ben was loud and big and always sat in a room like he was in charge of it. Francis was quiet and shy and never said more than he had to, but the way he smiled at Max made her feel he'd swung her into the air as well.

Then she noticed something on the verandah.

Ralph!

Ralph was Ben and Eleanor's dog. He was a hairy, smelly horse of an animal that never knew how to say hello without almost killing you, and after the last few days Max wasn't sure she could cope with a Ralph hello.

But amazingly, he trotted down the stairs and calmly sat beside her. That was it. No pushing, no knocking her to the ground, no rolling her in the dirt. And he didn't stink, either. In fact he smelled like a bathroom after a long shower with lots of shampoo.

"I knew you could do it!" Linden bolted from inside the house, ran down the stairs, and leaped into an all-out rumble with Ralph so that it was hard to see where Linden ended and the hairy rear end of Ralph began.

"You want us to leave you alone?" Max moved away from the churning ball of dust.

Linden turned his dirt-stained face toward her. "I've been training him."

"Well, when you've finished trying to prove Cro-Magnon

man still exists, you might want to say hello." Max's hands were firmly on her hips.

Linden stood up and tried to push his hair out of his eyes. He had this wild mop that always stuck out from his head like sails on an old ship. The hair sprung back, sending a small plume of dust swarming around his head. "Max!"

Then, in slow motion, Max saw Linden's body lunge toward her, angling in for a wide, all-embracing, farm-filled hug.

She had to stop him before he got any closer.

"What do you think you're doing?"

Ben, Francis, and Eleanor hid squirming smiles.

Linden stopped in mid–hug attempt, as if he'd run out of power. "Sorry. My brain must have gone into hibernation for a second there."

"Do you think it might wake up and join us sometime soon?" Max smirked.

"Anything's possible," Linden said with a smile that took over his face.

Max's mother finished another makeup routine in the car before opening her door and stepping out as if she were royalty. Ralph must have missed the "royal" bit, because his ears sprang up and he took a running jump at Max's mother, pushing her into a pile of leaves and grass that exploded into the air. He licked her face with a grime-covered, salivary tongue.

"Ralph!" Everyone flew to Max's mother's rescue.

Linden and Max grabbed Ralph as Ben, Eleanor, and Francis pushed away the leaves and helped Max's mother to her feet.

She stood up and tried to steady her high heels on the uneven ground. She looked like a cross between the bride of Frankenstein and a Barbie doll after a windstorm. When Max's mother stood next to Linden and Ralph, with their wild dust-filled hair and fur, the three of them looked like some freaky family photo.

Linden held on to Ralph's collar and wondered where his training had gone wrong. The rest of them waited for the explosion, but all Max's mother said was, "What an energetic dog."

She brushed herself down as Eleanor and Ben looked at each other. So did Ralph and Linden. Max's eyes drew half-closed in suspicion, wondering where her real mother was.

Linden resumed breathing, now he knew his life wasn't over. "Sorry about that, Mrs. Remy."

"Ms. Beckinsdale, actually." She picked some leaves from her hair. "It's fine."

Max's eyes widened. Since when had her mother started using her maiden name? It looked as if anything to do with Max's father was finished from now on.

Ben tried to lighten the situation with a little humor. "They spend lots of money in those Paris fashion shows to look like that."

Silence. Max's mother had no sense of humor, especially

when it came to how she looked. There was an awkward pause until finally she laughed. "Oh, Ben, you always were so funny."

Okay, Max thought, *where's my mother gone?* She was here before, but now she's been replaced by this wild-haired, merry-making loony.

"How about a cup of tea?" Ben asked, still seeming pleased with his joke.

At least she won't accept, thought Max. *She'll want to rush back to the city to wash off the country as fast as she can.*

"That'd be lovely," her mother said, pulling more leaves from her hair.

What! Max's mother never accepted an offer to come inside the house. Why now? And what was she going to say to people she'd hardly ever said hello to? Max's horror was interrupted by her mother's cell phone.

"Yes?" Pause. "Is he?" Pause. "Well, we'll see about that." She closed her phone abruptly. "A young network personality has decided to throw a tantrum at a major publicity event. I'm going to have to pass on the tea."

Saved! Max hurriedly escorted her mother to the car and quickly kissed her good-bye, before running back to Eleanor and Ben and diving into their arms as if they were human pools of chocolate. When Max turned to give her mother a final wave good-bye, she noticed her creased brow. A strange guilty feeling crept over her as her mother offered a small smile and drove away.

"Tea's still on if anyone wants it," Ben said eagerly. "There's cinnamon cake as well." Ben and Linden sped into the house, followed by a smiling Eleanor and Francis.

Max stood in the yard for a moment longer. Coming back to the farm made her feel like she was coming home. She felt the breeze wrap around her as she stared at it all. The shed, the paddocks, the—"Aaaaahhhh!"

Max swished her hands in front of her face in an attempt to drive away the sudden *whoosh* of squealing and screeching.

Then it stopped.

Max looked at her feet. Three small chicks were pecking the ground. Then she saw something else. Geraldine, the chicken who, Max swore, used her as target practice, had had babies.

"Training your kids to be just like you?" Max mumbled. Geraldine only clucked away.

"Remember, you're the chicken and I'm the human, which means I'm smarter than you." Max flicked her head and turned away in an "I-showed-you" kind of way, until her foot squelched into something soft and slippery. The three chicks had created a freshly laid pile of chicken poop before wobbling away to join their mom. The smell rose up and hit Max's nose with a firm whack. Her foot was covered in it.

"Thanks for the welcome-back gift," she snapped. "All of you." She found a patch of grass to wipe off their stinky handiwork before going into the house.

CHAPTER 4

A Secret Lab and a
Journey Through Time

When Ben had talked about cinnamon cake and tea, he'd forgotten to mention the dinner that came with it. Normally, Max couldn't understand how they could eat meals that seemed big enough to power a small energy plant, but she hadn't eaten anything since the sushi roll at lunchtime, so when the smells of a baked dinner wafted out of the kitchen, Max's appetite bit into her stomach like an overexcited chihuahua.

Mealtimes at Mindawarra were usually accompanied by the clanging and clattering of plates and cutlery, mingled with a sense of urgency that came with placing Ben and Linden in front of food. When they were up to their second helpings, Max had had enough of being patient. She needed to ask the one important question. "How's the Time and Space Machine?"

Ben had a mouthful of baked lamb, pumpkin, and gravy. Max watched him chew it slowly and swallow before he finally said, "Good." He smiled. "Want to try her out?"

Max knocked her tea cup across the table, where it somersaulted into the mashed potatoes. "Yeah! Sorry."

Ben wiped his napkin across his mouth. "Right, then. Follow me."

Ben led the way down the long, musty hall to the living room. He threw back a tattered rug to reveal a trapdoor, then he lifted the door and made his way down a set of spiraling metal stairs.

Max had no idea the room held anything more interesting than layers of dust. "What's down there?"

"The lab," Ben's voice came echoing back.

"Ben's shed was a good lab for a while, but we needed something more . . ." Francis tried to find the right word as he followed Ben. ". . . sophisticated."

"There's a lab under your house?" Max scowled.

"Yes. Wonderful, isn't it?" Eleanor made her way down the stairs.

"Why didn't anyone tell me?"

"They did. Just now," Linden answered as he too disappeared below.

Max took a deep breath. As much as she'd grown to love these people, they had an extremely annoying habit of staying calm in the face of amazing news.

When she stepped down into the lab, she immediately forgot her bad mood. It still had the usual messiness of Ben's old lab, but underneath the books and newspapers, goggles, boxes, tubes, and his miniature replica of Big Ben was a shiny, new lab. Above the polished white floor were chrome benches with beeping, humming lab equipment, but the most exciting bit was a large round platform in the center of the lab. Sitting under a soft pool of light was a glass cabinet that contained the new Time and Space Machine.

"Sorry about the mess." Ben picked up a lab coat and hung it on an already overcrowded hook. "But I think better this way."

"That's what he tells us, anyway," said Francis, putting the cap on a tube of glue.

Ben walked over to the platform and stood by the machine. "Come and look."

They all made their way past walls and tables covered with maps, diagrams and sketches of plans, strange devices, and indecipherable ideas.

Ben spoke as if he were a tour guide in an ancient museum. "After years of tireless research carried out by Eleanor, Francis, and me, we created the Matter Transporter, which, with the addition of the Time and Space Retractor Meter and the Aurora Stone that Francis discovered in Scotland, was developed into the device you now see before you—the Transporter Mark II, a machine that holds the dream of scientists throughout the centuries: the secret to time travel."

Eleanor and Linden burst into spontaneous applause as Francis blushed and again tried to find somewhere to put his hands. Ben beamed as if he'd just won the Nobel Prize.

"After making a few adjustments to the Time and Space Retractor Meter, we believe we've created the most efficient machine yet, and the good news for you, Max, is that we've fixed the glitch with the landings. From now on you should land exactly as you left."

"That's a relief." Linden rolled his eyes and sighed.

"What are you worried about? You always have the good landings," Max complained.

"Yeah, but now when we're on missions, I won't have a partner who smells like the back end of a sheep." Linden nodded as if he were simply stating the facts.

"Is that so. Well I—"

"But that's not all," Ben interrupted with more to reveal. "Francis?"

Francis nodded and spoke with a smaller, less award-winning voice than Ben's. "When Eleanor and I analyzed the chemical structure of the Aurora Stone, we knew its high-density energy supply would enable the Time and Space Machine to move at the speed of light, thus allowing time travel. But we had to conduct thorough testing to ensure the machine's safety before we could begin our first trials."

"When will you start the trials?" Max was eager to be one of the world's first time travelers.

"Last week," Ben said coolly.

"Last week?" Max's mind flooded with the questions that cascaded into her brain. "But how'd you . . . Where did you . . . What kind of . . . ?"

"You're really going to have to finish some of those questions if you want an answer," Linden advised before turning to Ben. "How'd it go?"

Ben looked at Francis and Eleanor. "I'd say it was a success."

"All right!" Linden's mind was already flicking through history, trying to choose which parts he wanted to see first.

Max stared, openmouthed. She remembered when she'd met Ben and Eleanor and thought they were a pair of chicken farmers, and how when she'd gone to London to find Francis, she'd thought he was a grumpy old man with bad taste in cardigans and baggy trousers. These same relatives, who looked like regular people, were not only superspies but now time travelers as well.

"Who went?" Linden asked, as Max still hadn't managed to close her mouth.

"Eleanor and I. Francis stayed here in the lab and monitored the test."

"Where'd you go?"

"Norway in the Middle Ages." Eleanor smiled. "I have always had a soft spot for Norway."

"What was it like being able to travel through time?" Max had unraveled her brain, regained control over her mouth, and finally managed a question.

Eleanor thought about this carefully. "It's like history gets on with doing what it's doing and we get to see it up close as it's happening."

Her explanation short-circuited Max's brain again.

"Did you see . . . But how do you . . . Can you . . . ?"

"Let me help you out," Linden offered. "Can you touch things?"

"Not exactly. It's like walking around in a virtual movie," Eleanor clarified. "Objects do have a dimension, but we only experienced some of their mass, so that our hands slightly passed through the surface of them."

Linden's eyebrows arched. "So, if you can pick things up, does that mean you can change the past?"

Francis's face took on a serious look. "We think so, but we're working on a program to stop humans from being able to do just that. That is the one factor that makes the Time and Space Machine so brilliant and so dangerous. Even with the best intentions we're not sure of the ramifications."

"And in the wrong hands that function could prove disastrous," Ben warned. He'd changed from tour guide to Hollywood actor.

"Were you scared? Did anyone see you?" Linden imagined wielding a sword against knights twice his size.

"We've incorporated a protective coating into the machine that makes you invisible," Eleanor explained. "It'll be safer for you that way."

"And less freaky for the people you run into. You won't have to explain *when* you're from and how you got there," added Ben.

Linden moaned. "So the people of history won't get to see how good-looking I am. Doesn't seem fair to go all that way and not give them a thrill."

"They'll get over it." Ben ruffled Linden's wild hair.

"How does it work?" Max was keen to get to the part where she could use it.

Francis took the Transporter Mark II out of the cabinet as if it were a rare gem.

"Much the same as when you transport through space. You write the destination on the LCD screen using the rod at the side, but add the extra dimension of time. Say or write 'Transport,' and, provided the address exists, you will be transported directly."

It sounded too simple. "Is that it?" Max's face creased into a frown.

"Yep. Now that it has the power of the Aurora Stone." Ben hitched up his trousers. "And when you want to return to the place you transported from, simply write 'Return' on the screen."

"Can we try it now?" Max asked.

"Do you feel up to it?" Ben looked at her sternly.

Max straightened up, her chin tucked in, her eyes firm, her mind buzzing with the fact that she was facing one of the most important moments of her life. One to be taken seriously. One to be faced with bravery, dignity, and courage.

"What, are you crazy?" she blustered as her hands flew to her hips. "I've waited for this moment ever since I heard about the Time and Space Machine. I've lived for this moment for a whole year. It's amazing I stayed even half-sane just thinking about it!"

"I'd take that as a yes," Linden translated.

"Where would you like to go?" Ben asked her, as if he were driving a tour bus.

Max went to open her mouth, but Linden cut her off. "Prehistory," he blurted. "With dinosaurs. Maybe Late Jurassic."

"Prehistory it is." The air tingled with night-before-Christmas jitters.

Francis gently handed Max the Transporter Mark II and a leather belt with a pouch and gold clasp in the middle. "We've had this special belt made that's lined with titanium. It will keep the machine safe. Time travel can be a rough ride."

Max put on the belt and nestled the transporter snugly inside.

Ben started to get this funny look on his face, kind of scrunched up like he was about to cry. "You may feel a bit funny when you land. Make sure you give yourselves a few minutes to adjust."

"Right." Max entered the destination on the LCD screen.

"It's like you're bending time, making it different from how we know it."

"Excellent." Linden imagined it before him.

"And make sure your visit lasts no longer than five minutes," Ben said, and sniffed.

"Okay." Max took Linden's hand before Ben could say any more.

"And be careful. . . ."

Max said, "Transport," and left her uncle's sentence floating in midair as she and Linden were flung through space and time back to somewhere in prehistory.

CHAPTER 5

A Bad Case of
Dinosaur Poop

Max and Linden appeared in a flash of fluorescent light with tiny sparks of color falling around them like fireworks. They hung suspended in the air for a few seconds before floating gently onto the thick grass of a vast escarpment.

"Now, that's what I call a ride." Linden's unruly hair had become even more unruly and his shirt and pants were twisted round his body.

"Yeah." Max's dazed brain nestled beneath her hair, which was standing on end and swaying from side to side in the breeze.

In the past when they'd transported through space, it had felt like being picked up by a giant hand and placed somewhere else. Traveling through time felt more like being flung into a long twisting tunnel at a million miles an hour by a giant as big as Jupiter.

Until they stopped.

Small bubbles of images floated in front of them, reforming bit by bit, until a picture of where they were formed around them. A lush rain forest spread out below them, with a clear blue sky above. There were vivid green trees, huge ferns, and large pools of clear rippling water. And there was something else.

"Can you smell something?" Linden was having trouble getting his clothes to cooperate with his body.

"Maybe this is how prehistory smelled," Max said as she winced. "Which would be just my luck."

Linden was trying to focus on the object forming next

to him. "Or maybe we landed right next to a . . . a . . . huge pile of dinosaur poop." His hand flew to his nose as the breeze smacked a soured whiff into his face.

"Dinosaur poop?" Max said nasally as she held her nose too. "We're in the middle of prehistory, I've got the whole world to land in, and I'm sitting next to a pile of poop the size of a house."

Linden looked around in awe as the last of their surroundings pieced itself into place. He was standing in one of his favorite parts of history with a giant pterodactyl swooping over his head. "Wow!" he breathed.

Max watched as its huge wings whomped through the air and flew away. Then her eyes widened. "What's that?"

Linden looked behind them and saw a greenish stony wall. "It looks like . . . like . . ." Then he realized. "It's the rear end of a dinosaur, and I think he's about to let another one go!"

An enormous bulge of brown disgusting mush appeared and fell toward them.

"Aaaaahhhh!" They rolled quickly down the embankment only just escaping the deathly poop splat but not its squelchy spray.

"Oooph!" Max's roll was stopped by the trunk of a giant tree fern. "Errr! Even at the dawn of time I can't last five minutes without bashing into something."

She pushed herself away from the trunk and saw her hand partially soak into the outside layer.

"It's just like Eleanor said!"

Her amazement was cut short by the whiff of poop splattered on her.

She untangled herself from the fronds, took out a hanky, and wiped down her clothes. "Why couldn't we go somewhere less smelly for our first journey through time?"

Linden looked up from the grassy mound that had stopped his roll.

"Max?"

"Or somewhere where I wasn't welcomed by giant lumps of yesterday's lunch."

"Max?"

"We had the whole of history to choose from, but you wanted to go to the land of the dinosaurs. What's so fascinating about a bunch of old stegosauruses anyway?"

"Apatosauruses, actually. Previously known as brontosauruses. One of the largest land animals ever to have existed. We're in the Late Jurassic period."

Max was trying to wipe a stubborn piece of muck from her jacket. "I don't care what period we're in as long as it doesn't slime me again." She frowned. "Great. Now there's a really hot breeze."

"It's not a breeze." Linden had this strange look in his eye. Max followed his gaze. Rising out of the tree ferns, the apatosaurus had stretched out its long neck and was hovering over Max as if she were an ant under a microscope. Its teeth were as long as she was tall, and its nostrils were like two openings into very warm, very smelly caves.

Max did the only thing she could.

She turned and ran.

"Max!" Linden cried, but she didn't hear him. The beast lumbered after her with great leaden thumps. Max leaped over thick roots, skirted around ponds, and scrambled across fallen moss-covered tree trunks.

"Please, don't let my life end in the jaws of an animal that doesn't exist."

"Max!" Linden called again, but it was no good. She couldn't hear him. The pasta-whatever-a-saurus was bearing down on her, thumping its way toward her inevitable and premature demise. Very premature. Like two hundred million years before she was even born.

Then she saw her escape. She ran toward a small cave, and with the prehistoric giant toe seconds away from delivering certain death, she scrambled through its narrow entrance.

Max heaved and panted and sank into the muddy floor of the cave as the dinosaur thumped by. She wiped a muddied hand across her forehead and smiled. Ben and Eleanor had made time travel sound safe, but luckily Max had used her wit and intelligence to outsmart the giant lizard.

"Hi." Linden appeared at the mouth of the cave.

"Did you manage to give the dinosaur the slip too?" Max gasped as mud started seeping through her pants.

"No, he kept running toward the large fern he was

heading for," Linden said. "Apatosauruses are herbivores. Don't take it personally, but he wouldn't have eaten you if you'd been roasted and served with gravy."

"I knew that." Max's feeling of victory slipped away.

"And they can't see us," Linden reminded her. "We're invisible, remember?"

Now she felt really silly. She squeezed through the cave mouth and stood her poop- and mud-stained self next to a clean-looking Linden. "How can you be sure? Ben and Eleanor don't know everything about time travel yet."

Linden walked toward the dinosaur. "Hey, big fella, look at me." He danced between the dinosaur's toes as bits of fern it was munching fell around him. "Hey, lizard-breath! Why don't you take that big toe of yours and get rid of me?"

"All right, you've made your point." Max sulked, but when Linden offered her a huge grin, she softened. "That's all my stomach can handle of your dance moves, anyway."

Max looked at her watch. "It's time to go back."

"I'm not sure I've had a good look around yet." Linden gazed at the nearby lagoon and waterfall and the thick jungle with crocodiles, turtles, and all kinds of flying pterosaurs he'd never heard or read about.

Then he saw Max. She gave him a look that said she was done. "Actually, maybe I am ready," he reconsidered.

Max opened the clasp of the belt with the Transporter Mark II and wrote "*return*" on the screen. As she grabbed

Linden's hand, they saw the apatosaurus drop another huge poop before walking off into the sunset.

"He must have had curry for dinner," Linden chuckled. Max said, "Transport," and they were gone.

Ben, Eleanor, and Francis watched anxiously as the time travelers appeared from a flash of sparks and fluorescent light and floated before them.

"They're back!" Ben cried.

Max and Linden hovered in the air before safely coming in to land. Ben ran at them, his face a flood of smiles and tears. His arms flung open like a singer from an old musical welcoming home a long-lost son.

Until he smelled something.

"What's that smell?" He stopped dead.

"We had some problems with a dinosaur and a deadly case of diarrhea," Linden whispered as Ben sniffed at Max's muddied look.

"Oh." Ben sighed guiltily. "I was sure we'd fixed the landings."

"The landing was the cleanest part, it was everything after that got messy." Linden smirked until he caught Max's expression, which made him feel like a cat that had just lost one of its nine lives.

"Congratulations!" Eleanor clasped her hands. "You did it!"

"How was it?" quizzed Francis.

"It was incredible. When can we go again?" Linden could hardly ask fast enough.

"Max?" Ben sensed her bad mood.

"It was great," she said unenthusiastically. "I just don't get why even in the middle of prehistory I have this habit of attracting filth."

Ben smiled. "Let's get you upstairs so you can clean up. Then I want to hear all about it."

Linden began talking rapidly as Francis put the Transporter Mark II safely away and they all made their way upstairs. Max followed slowly behind, and as she reached the top of the stairs, she turned toward the glowing cabinet. A smile curved into her lips. She'd done it. She'd traveled through time, and apart from a little dinosaur poop and some prehistoric mud, she couldn't wait to do it again.

CHAPTER 6

An Important
Phone Call

Chronicles of Spy Force:

Max Remy and Alex Crane stood on the command deck of the starship *Intrepid Voyager* and carefully scrutinized the scanner. A small green dot bleeped innocently on the darkened screen before them, but what it indicated was anything but innocent. It was an asteroid, traveling at the speed of light, and it was headed straight for them.

"What do you think?" Max leaned over the shoulder of the ship's navigator.

"I've studied all the available data, and I estimate we have a 97 percent chance of a direct collision course."

"And the size of the asteroid?" Agent Crane asked.

The navigator gasped as if he weren't getting enough air. "About the size of Mars."

Max saw the edge of Alex's face flicker. She'd never once seen Alex afraid, but that flicker gave away a moment Max would never forget.

"How long have we got?"

The navigator wiped his brow with an already soggy hanky. "About twelve minutes."

Alex turned to Max. "How are the repairs on the Astro-Thruster going?"

The Astro-Thruster was a device that used high-frequency signals to destroy objects in the starship's path. It had been damaged in battle with a rebel ship two days ago.

"Slow. The technicians are working by remote, and the

solar activity outside the ship is interfering with the speed at which they can work."

The Astro-Thruster was the only device capable of obliterating an asteroid of this size. There was no alternative. "We'll do it manually."

Within sixty seconds the two agents were standing in the sealed exit chamber in preparation for their entry into space. Their suits had been checked and the oxygen cable fastened. If all went well, they should be able to reach the Astro-Thruster, repair the damage, and be back on the command deck in time to see one of the most spectacular explosions of their careers. Alex looked across at Max and gave her a wink before turning to the Chamber Master and giving the nod.

The doors of the chamber opened and they were flung into space. Max loved this part. It was like floating in a giant ocean of stars, and even though they faced possible death, it somehow made her feel calm.

Alex reached the Thruster first and immediately began repairing the damage. She worked fast and without fear. She'd almost finished when, with only ninety seconds left before impact, a violent force slammed her into the side of the ship. Max avoided the same treatment by grabbing hold of the Astro-Thruster. She radioed her friend who hung limply in her suit.

"Alex? Can you hear me?"

No response. Max took the tools from Alex's hands

and began working, unsure when another blast of solar wind would come her way. She had to work fast and then get her friend inside. She had to save the *Intrepid Voyager* from being pulverized into a million pieces of space junk. From

"Aaaaahhhh!" A blast of wind slammed into Max's face. She looked up from her bench on the verandah and saw the spinning blades of an upright fan whirring like a swarm of angry wasps.

"Thought you might like a little breeze." Ben failed to notice Max's pale expression as he sat next to her. "Yeah, that's better." He smiled as Max tried to calm her heart rate.

At Ben and Eleanor's house, the verandah was Max's special place to sit and write or to talk about things. She didn't know if it was the acres of land stretching off toward the faraway horizon, or the birds flitting in and out of the trees, or the smell of paddocks and Ben and Eleanor's cooking that made it so perfect. No matter how crazy the world was, sitting on the verandah made everything seem calm and tranquil.

Most of the time.

"Larry's been at some clay making today," Ben announced.

When conversations started with Larry the pig, Max usually regretted asking questions. She loved her aunt and uncle, but predicting the weather from the behavior of their pig was too close to crazy. *Don't ask anything*, Max's brain warned her mouth.

"Clay making?" Max winced. Why didn't she listen to her brain?

"Yeah. On really hot days he digs up clay and nudges small models out of them. The sun bakes them rock hard. Gotta be a hot day, though."

This was too much. "Models?"

"Yeah. Once he made a model that was the spitting image of the president."

They sat in silence for a few minutes before he stood up. "Think I might go and check on Geraldine and her chicks."

Max smiled as she watched him leave. She picked up her book, but before she could start writing again, Eleanor stuck her head around the door. "Knock, knock. Can I join you?"

"Sure." Max closed her book. She'd finish her Alex Crane adventure later.

"Thanks for visiting." Eleanor brushed Max's hair from her eyes. "It's lovely to have you back. Always feels like you belong here."

Max's skin rippled with goose bumps. Her aunt could do that with just a few words. Max tried to think of something to say in return, to tell her she felt the same. She scrabbled through her brain but came up with nothing. "Eleanor? How was it possible that I wrote stories about Alex and Spy Force before I even knew they existed?"

Max's aunt smiled and leaned back against the wooden bench.

"I was wondering when you were going to ask that. When you were little, you stayed with us while your mom and dad went on a vacation together. You were a curious little thing, and one day I found you in the study sitting inside a giant cardboard storage box holding a photo in one hand and a medallion in the other."

"The photo was of Alex and her dad," Max guessed.

"Yes, and the medallion was from Spy Force. You wanted to know who the girl in the photo was, and I told you she was one of the bravest people I'd ever known. They both were. I put the photo and medallion away, and you never asked anything about them again. I guess what you'd seen stayed with you long after that day."

"Did Alex change after her dad . . . died?"

"She was quieter and more serious, but was still terribly brave."

Max's chest tightened at the thought of anything terrible ever happening to her dad. She shook off a chilled shiver.

"Did you enjoy your time as a spy?"

Her aunt's eyes glistened. "I hadn't felt truly alive until

I joined Spy Force. I'd always dreamed of a life full of spies and adventures, but I never thought it could happen. Then, a few months later, things got even better." She grinned cheekily. "I met Ben. The smartest, sweetest, best-looking man I'd ever known."

"Were you scared when you went on missions?"

"A little, at first, but Ben and I made a good team and it just . . . felt right." Eleanor looked at her niece. "Like you and Linden."

Max could feel her cheeks redden.

"When you find a great partner, always remember that you have something special." She looked across the yard at Ben, who was holding one of the chicks to his cheek. "Not everyone knows."

Max thought about the missions she and Linden had been on. They did make a good team, and even though he joked way too much, she trusted him.

"How's your mom?" asked Eleanor.

As sisters Eleanor and Max's mom rarely spoke and had never been close. Max knew little about her family and was five years old before she even knew she had an aunt.

"She's good. She's getting married." Max had done such a good job of blocking it out, she'd almost forgotten. Then she remembered the worst part.

"And Dad invited me to visit him in California, but Mom wants me to stay here and help with the wedding."

Max slowly twisted the pen in her hand. Even though she'd traveled through time, she'd give it all back if she could visit her dad. She'd even give up being in Spy Force.

"When were you supposed to go?"

"He said I could come over right away."

Eleanor looked thoughtful. "You know what? I think it's time I called your mother." She kissed Max on the head and went inside the house.

What did she mean? What was she going to say? What if they had a fight and never spoke again? What if Max was never allowed back to Mindawarra? She had to stop Eleanor. She ran inside just as her aunt spoke into the receiver, "Hello there."

Max dropped into a chair in the kitchen. She tried to listen in, but Eleanor faced away and her words were all muffled. Besides, Max could tell from the little Eleanor did say, her mother was doing most of the talking.

"Please, please, please," Max recited. "Don't let it end badly."

The phone call seemed to last forever, until suddenly Eleanor hung up. Max froze, not wanting the next moments of her life to happen. She looked into the hall, and the light in Eleanor's study went on. *It must have been bad*, Max thought. *She can't even face me*.

Max sat back on the chair as she heard Eleanor make another phone call. She didn't bother trying to listen. There wasn't going to be anything good about hearing

Eleanor plead with her mom, but after a few moments she hung up and phoned someone else.

Who was she talking to?

Max didn't have to wait long to find out.

"That was the longest chat I've had with your mom in years," said Eleanor. "Funny old thing. You know—"

Max couldn't stand it any longer. "Eleanor, what happened?"

"Oh, sorry, dear. Your mother said yes. Now, do you think you might have room for some pumpkin pie?"

Pie? Eleanor had possibly told Max one of the most important sentences in the history of the world, and all she could talk about was pie?

"Did someone say pie?" Linden appeared out of nowhere, which he did on a regular basis, especially at the mention of food.

"Max and I were going to have some. Are you in?"

Eleanor bustled into cupboards, collecting plates and forks.

"But how did you do it?" persisted Max.

"Ben and I have been invited to speak at a conference in LA in a few weeks, and I convinced your mother to let you travel with us. I've checked the flight and there are plenty of seats left."

"But the wedding?" Max had to make sure she'd heard right.

"It's not for months. I told her you'd be back in plenty

of time for that. Oh, and you have to get ahead with your schoolwork before you can go."

Max hoped this was all true and not some cruel nightmare she was in the middle of. "That's great!"

"What's great?" Ben walked into the kitchen, followed by Francis.

"Max is coming to California with us, and we're having pie. Want some?"

"Only if you made it," Francis said as Ben grabbed some plates and Eleanor scooped out the pieces of pie. Max could hear them chatting about how Eleanor had made it, but she understood none of it. She felt as if she were in one of those films where something good happens and corny music starts to play, flowers fall from the sky, and the world becomes full of light. She didn't care for girlie sparkles, and she'd never be caught dead in a situation like that, but for now she didn't care. She was going to be with her dad.

"Oh," Eleanor added almost as an afterthought. "We thought Linden could keep you company, if that's okay with you both. I've called your dad, Linden, and it's okay with him if you'd like to go."

"Sure." Linden scooped out another spoonful of pie.

"Max? Is that okay by you?"

It was more than okay. Max would love Linden to meet her dad and couldn't think of one other person she'd rather go on vacation with. Of course, she wasn't going to let Linden know that. "Yeah. Okay."

"It'll be nice to see your dad again. We always got along so well."

Max smiled at her aunt. Even hard things got sorted out in this house as if they were no big deal.

"Oh, Max." Ben wiped his napkin across his lips. "I forgot to give you this."

He pulled a small brown parcel out of his pocket.

Max tore off the paper. After undoing the strings that held closed a leather pouch, her face brightened. It was as if she were looking at a favorite toy from when she was a kid.

"We wanted you to have it," Eleanor said in a voice like a warm blanket. "We put it back together and upgraded it from the original. It's quieter now when you use it."

"After all," Ben added, "you helped make it possible, and now that you're a Spy Force agent, it might come in handy."

Max looked at the original Time and Space Machine cradled in her hands. All the memories of their first mission to London filled her head like an overflowing bath. There was an engraving on the back, which read:

Happy traveling, Max
Love, B & E

"Thanks." Her voice cracked and her lips flew shut.

"You're welcome." Ben sighed happily and turned to the others. "Larry's been making models again today."

As talk turned to models he'd made in the past, Larry grunted from the end of the yard as if he knew he was being spoken about.

Max held the Matter Transporter carefully in her hands. After all that had happened in the last few days, today had been a good day. Max sat back in her chair, surrounded by her favorite people in the world, and as she thought about visiting her dad, Larry snorted in the dark and pushed clay into strange shapes.

CHAPTER 7

Bon Voyage

Max sat on a bench in the school playground and counted the number of days in her notebook until she'd be on her way to California. She'd thought about visiting her dad so much over the years that she wondered whether she'd wake up like all the other times and realize they were still separated by endless oceans, slimy sea creatures, and a neurotic mother.

"Hey." Toby Jennings sat down next to her and opened his lunch box.

Max quickly closed her notebook. "What are you doing here?"

"Having my lunch," Toby answered innocently.

Max stared at him suspiciously. "You're not going to ask me why I'm sitting with all my friends?"

"Why would I want to do that when you're sitting alone?" He took a bite from a hefty-looking sandwich.

"Because that's the kind of thing you've said to me every day since I started at Hollingdale."

Max felt as if she were talking to a Toby look-alike or a Toby who had had his memory erased and forgotten that they weren't friends.

"Oh, Max." He sniffed. "Were you writing more of those stories?"

Max tried to stop her mouth from answering Toby's questions. There was something eerie about his knowing anything about her life.

"No. I mean, yeah." She instantly tried to put her book in her bag. Its tattered cover, which was held together by sticky tape, was the result of Toby having fought her for it a few months before. She tried to push it in farther, but it fell at Toby's feet.

"I'll get it." He leaned down to pick up the notebook and noticed one entry written in bright red. "You're going to California?"

"Yes." Max stared at her book trapped in Toby's hands. She had to get it from him, but just as she was about to pounce, he did something weird. He handed it back.

"Excellent. Where are you going to stay?"

"With my dad in LA." Now Max was really confused. Toby never handed anything back to anyone without making them beg for it. Max slipped her notebook in her bag, and it was then that Toby noticed the leather pouch.

Max had to get out of there. Life was creepy enough living with her mother, but suddenly that felt normal compared with how Toby was behaving.

"Gotta go. See ya." She pulled her bag to her chest and moved speedily away.

Toby watched her go. *California, eh?* Toby thought. *And I'll bet there's something special in that pouch. I think it's time to do a little investigating.*

After lunch there was sport, so every student had to put their bag in their locker. This meant Max and her bag would be apart long enough for Toby to pay a visit.

"Mrs. Flagbottom, I don't feel very well."

Toby grabbed his stomach as the gym teacher came over to see what was wrong. He'd also dabbed his face with a faint layer of powder he kept in his bag for emergencies. Toby loved gym, so he'd never be suspected of faking an illness to get out of it.

"You certainly don't look well." Mrs. Flagbottom held his chin, saw his pale complexion, and fell for it.

"No, Ma'am."

"Go to the infirmary and lie down for a while."

A kid called Grace with wild orange hair, fluoro braces, and an annoying habit of skipping everywhere she went, skipped alongside Toby to sick bay. He lay on the bed and watched Grace skip her way back out the door. When she'd gone, he went to the lockers and easily picked Max's lock. He opened her bag and saw the communication device Max had been speaking into. Up close it looked like a minicomputer.

"Welcome to your new owner." Toby grinned, but when he pressed the same keys Max had, nothing happened. He checked for a power switch but gave up when he saw something else: Max's notebook.

"Now I'll find out what you've been up to."

Toby put the communication device back in Max's bag and flicked through the pages of her book. They were crammed with stories of rescues from erupting volcanoes, escapes from menacing thugs, descriptions of flying backpacks called PFDs, and flying through the sky at hyperspeeds in an invisible jet.

"This stuff can't be real," he muttered, but there was something about the way the stories were written that made him think they were true. He then read about her trip to Mindawarra to test the new Time and Space Machine. His face swelled into a bulging smile as if he'd been stung by an ingenious idea. "This machine sounds too good to waste on Max."

He put the notebook back in her bag and reached for the leather pouch. "Now, what do we have here?" He undid the string that held it closed and pulled out a purple box-shaped device. It had a sensor at the top, an LCD screen above a computer-like keypad, and three keys labeled "Scan," "Activate," and "Transport." There was a rod at the side and a green light labeled "Power."

"This must be the Time and Space Machine," he whispered excitedly. "It's a little daggy looking, but if it's going to fly me round the world I guess I can live with that."

With his brilliant idea whirring inside his head, Toby carefully placed the machine into his own bag and, finding Max's address book, wrote down where her father lived. Then he heard footsteps at the other end of the corridor. He had to be quick. He searched through his bag until he found a small block of wood from his woodworking class. The footsteps came closer. He slipped the wood into the pouch, tied it up, and replaced it in Max's bag just in time to slip around a corner and watch Principal Peasers hum past in a haze of hippie love.

A smug smile appeared on Toby's lips as he watched her walk away. He'd be good at this spy work, and deep in his heart he knew that Max would be overjoyed that he'd decided to join her. He crept back to sick bay with a warm feeling circling in his stomach, knowing life was about to get very, very exciting.

CHAPTER 8

Desert Death Trap
and a Long-Awaited
Reunion

Chronicles of Spy Force:

They were the best father-daughter team in Spy Force since Alex Crane and her dad. They'd beaten baddies in Botswana, fought criminals in the Pacific, and captured kidnappers in Kalimantan. They were tough and smart and always knew what the other was thinking without having to say it. Max sat in the passenger side of the desert buggy with a map fluttering on her lap.

"The hotel should be . . ."

". . . coming up on our right," her dad answered above the noise of the engine.

Max smiled. "Yeah."

They were in the Sahara Desert, in the sand-swept and majestic country of Algeria. The temperature had reached 118 degrees Fahrenheit, and the hot, dry wind was wrapping itself around them like layers of invisible heated blankets.

A faint dot of green appeared in the distance, and as they approached they knew they'd found it: the oasis they were searching for. Surrounded by imposing mountains of sand and sweeping stretches of dry golden plains was a lush eruption of rich green trees, shrubs, and palms.

Cool air poured over them as they drove along the tree-lined road to the Hotel d'Algiers, tucked in the center of the oasis. They stopped before a fountain at the entrance and were offered drinks while porters scurried to unload their bags.

"We have to keep our eyes open," Max's father whispered through half-closed lips. "Malovic is very cunning and if he catches wind of our plan . . ."

". . . it'll put a nasty edge on our Saharan adventure."

Max's father smiled. Her courage astounded him, and he couldn't imagine a father more proud of his daughter than he was.

They'd been sent to capture the dreaded Alphonso Malovic, a wizened old man who leaned over a cane and hummed as he walked, but beneath his flowing robes, wrinkled skin, and off-key tunes was the most conniving racketeer the desert had ever seen. Malovic had contacts all over the world, and whatever anyone needed, no matter how sinister, he could obtain it. It had taken months to organize, but they'd finally set up a meeting with Malovic to discuss a phony business proposition they had for him.

Malovic's assistants insisted they freshen up before the meeting and took them to a private bathing room decorated in intricate mosaics. They sat on a tiled bench in their swimsuits as steam surged from tiny jets embedded in the wall, and water trickled from fountains all around them. After a long journey through the Saharan heat, this was exactly what they needed.

Until what happened next. Several clicking sounds reverberated throughout the room as metal plates slipped across the drains. The trickling water became hissing streams, bursting into the room in angry torrents.

"What's happening?" called Max.

"It's a double cross," her father yelled back as the water rose around their ankles. He raced to the door, but it had been bolted shut. The water quickly rose so high that it lifted them from their feet and floated them toward the ceiling.

Max desperately looked for a way out. The gap between the ceiling and the rising water became a sliver with barely enough room to breathe. What were they going to do? How where they going to escape? Would this be the end of Max and her dad? She'd be able to save them in an instant if only she had some

"Drinks? Peanuts?"

Max jumped as a stewardess with bright red lips and overly straight teeth leaned in and bellowed at her.

"No, thanks." Max reeled from being wrenched so abruptly out of the Sahara.

"Peanuts?" Ben snapped awake from a deep sleep. Max was sure her uncle could wake up from a coma if food were mentioned. "Love some."

Max closed her book. She'd started writing to take her mind off her convulsing stomach, which was threatening to fly out of her mouth and leave her body forever at any second. She wasn't sure if her queasiness was due to the flight, the foil-covered trays with what she suspected was food, or the fact that she was going to see her dad again. *And* his new wife. Max's . . . *stepmother*. She'd never faced the word before, even in her head. Other kids had stepmothers and stepfathers—kids from books and TV—and they hardly ever got a good rap. What was she going to be like? What if Max didn't like her? Or what if she didn't like Max?

She held her stomach as a new wave of sickness rolled over her.

"Nervous?" Ben munched on his peanuts as he studied the scowl on Max's face. "I am too. Never was a big fan of flying."

"The flying part's okay," Max answered quietly.

"Oh." Ben nodded, then held out his arm. "Pinch me."

"Sorry?"

"Pinch me. Go on. I can take it."

Max's aunt and uncle could be odd, and sometimes it was better not to question what they said. She reached out and pinched him.

"Ouch!" Ben rubbed his arm. "See?"

Max was confused. "See what?"

"You really are on your way to see your dad."

Max laughed. Ben was sweet in his loopy kind of way. He looked around conspiratorially. "I'm nervous about who we're meeting too." He lowered his voice even further. "Can I tell you a secret?"

Max's eyes widened. "Yeah."

"We're having a meeting with Harrison to show him the new Time and Space Machine."

"Harrison?"

"Shhhh. It's a secret. At least I hope it still is." Then he added guiltily, "Hope the machine treats Harrison better than it treated you."

"It wasn't the machine's fault, it's brilliant." She paused.

Ben smiled. "We'll be there soon." He rubbed his arm where Max had pinched it. "You've sure got some grip." He ruffled her hair, put on his headphones, and began flicking through the channels on the screen in front of him.

Max felt the pouch in her bag for the hundredth time since she'd left home, to make sure the original Time and Space Machine Ben and Eleanor had given her was still there. A voice then announced they were beginning their descent. Ben grabbed Max's fidgeting hand to reassure her that everything was going to be okay but also to stop her from picking the end of her sweater to bits. She'd already pulled a packet of tissues apart, which lay around her feet like a mini–paper snowstorm.

Before much time had passed, they were in the terminal of the airport being pushed around by waves of people frantically moving in all directions. Eleanor and Ben grabbed Max's and Linden's hands and made their way to the luggage carousel. After they'd piled their bags onto carts, Max and Linden stood on a seat and searched the crowd for Max's dad.

"What's he look like?" Linden asked.

Max fished a photo out of her pocket. "It's a bit old, but he probably hasn't changed much."

The terminal was a frenzy of announcements, flight calls, carts of food and luggage, and all sorts of people from jocks to vacationers, businesspeople, and a group of Tibetan monks.

"Is there anyone *not* in this terminal today?" Linden shouted to Max over the noise, but then he noticed a man caught in a tangle of schoolkids who had flooded around his legs. "Is that him?"

Max looked to where Linden was pointing and saw the man dancing through the kids as if they were baby chicks he was trying not to squash.

"That's him," she breathed.

The man looked up, stopped dancing, and let out the same big smile Max remembered. He wore a floppy sweater and baggy trousers, and his hair fell in mismatched waves above red-rimmed glasses.

"Max!" he called out above the chaos.

Max had pictured meeting up with her dad so many times, now that it was really happening it seemed so . . . so . . . normal.

He ran toward her, scooped her off the seat, and swung her through the air like he'd done when she was a kid. Linden stood back as two men in business suits ducked and scowled, only narrowly avoiding being slugged by flying shoes. Max held on to her dad partly so she wouldn't fly into the crowd but mostly so she could make sure he was real.

He stopped twirling and pulled her in tight. "Boy, have I missed you."

"Ahem," Ben interrupted after even more hugging. "When you two are finished, we'd like to say hello as well."

Max's father laughed and put her down. The two men threw their arms around each other so vigorously it looked as if they were going to wrestle each other to the ground. He then hugged Eleanor, whose face creased into a half smile, half frown.

"Still as beautiful as ever," Max's dad said. "Beats me how you got stuck with Ben."

"She could have done worse," Ben shot back. "She could have married you."

The two men laughed while Eleanor lit up in a bright blush. She wriggled out of the hug and placed her hands on Linden's shoulders. "And this is Linden."

Max's dad's smile got bigger. "You have no idea how these folks rave about you."

Linden looked away self-consciously. "I have a rough idea."

Max nervously scanned the area around them. Her dad instantly knew who she was looking for. "Mee Lin had to work today and will join us later. For now, let's go home and start the party."

He gripped Max's hand tightly as he led them to his

chauffeur-driven car. "Don't worry," he whispered so no one else could hear. "She's going to love you."

In the car Max's dad, Ben, and Eleanor chatted noisily about lots of old and mostly funny times. Max and Linden listened and laughed at their wild stories as they crisscrossed LA through a labyrinth of highways, and flew past its billboards and people and music and traffic. They didn't notice any of it.

The city fell away into the background as the car threaded its way along a winding, tree-lined road, and when the house finally appeared, it was as if they'd all been driven into a movie.

Linden stared at the multilevel mansion. "If I open my eyes, will I wake up?"

"It's not as big as it looks," Max's dad said modestly as he showed them inside.

But it was. Set on a hill surrounded by a forest of trees, flowers, and fountains, the house had twelve bedrooms, five bathrooms, and a garden with a pond and waterfall nestled in the middle.

Linden whispered to Max, "Are you sure this is your dad?"

Max looked admiringly at her father as he laughed with Ben and Eleanor. "Yep. I'm sure."

"Excellent," Linden replied thankfully. "I was worried that someone would tell us we'd been picked up by the wrong guy."

There weren't many things that could do it, but the

sight of Linden's room made him go completely silent. He looked at the enormous bed, the windows overlooking the pond, and his own bathroom with spa. He opened his mouth but nothing came out.

"You're welcome, Linden." Max's dad smiled. "It's great to finally meet you."

Max was shown to her room last. Before he left her to settle in, her father squatted in front of her. "I've been looking forward to this for so long I was beginning to think it would never happen." His eyes moistened as if he were about to cry, something Max usually ran from, but as he gently pulled her in for another hug, she could have stayed there forever.

"I've got to do some work for tomorrow's shoot." He strode toward the door and turned. "I want you to treat this as your home, Max. I'll be in the study if you need me."

He raised his fingers to his lips and blew her a kiss. Max caught it and put it in her pocket, just like she used to do when she was a kid.

"For later," he said, and gave her a wink as he turned away.

Max sank onto her bed, her body a mixture of tingling and fatigue. Her dad could always make even a normal day seem like a party. When they'd lived together, the house was always full of people, and even when they'd just moved into a new house, it'd be filled that evening with music, food, and new neighbors. The parties ran long into the night, while Max lay on the couch, slipping in and out of sleep. She'd refuse to go to bed in case she missed the fun, but every time, she'd wake up in her dad's arms as he carried her to her room. Her mother would complain about the chaos, but secretly Max could see she loved it. Max's dad would grab her mom and twirl her, and within seconds her parents would be laughing and kissing like two people who would always be in love.

"Must be hard having your parents live so far apart."

Max sat up. It was Linden. He had this ability of always knowing exactly what she was thinking. She looked away as she realized there were tears on her face.

She was about to give him a well-crafted and witty reply, but something caught in her throat and she couldn't say anything. Linden saw her reddened eyes and knew exactly what she needed. "Swim?"

Max nodded.

"Excellent. The pond's heated and has a slide and a floating stereo." Linden grabbed Max by the hand and pulled her to a standing position. "We're only here for a short while, so we can't waste a second."

Max smiled. It wasn't every day you met people like Linden, and even if he was a little pushy, life always seemed so much better when he was around.

CHAPTER 9

A Meeting and a
Pink Nightmare

"Max." Her dad rubbed his hands together, both nervous and excited. "I'd like you to meet your stepmother."

He stood aside from her bedroom door like a game-show host revealing the major prize. Max straightened her clothes and pushed back her hair for the millionth time.

A long, slender hand appeared from around the door frame, decorated with rings of gold and diamonds. Suddenly what Max was wearing felt all wrong. She wanted to run to the bathroom and pretend she wasn't there, but it was too late. The woman stepped into the room. A golden light surrounded her tall, elegant body. Max felt like a fish pulled out of the sea. She gulped and gawped and wished someone would throw her back. How could her dad have had a daughter with so little charm, so little elegance, devoid of any hint of style? A fashionless, bumbling—

"Max?"

Her eyes flicked open, and she tried to focus on where she was.

Big bed. Fluffy pillows. Strange room.

"Max, are you awake?" A voice came from the other side of the door. Then she remembered. She was at her dad's house in Hollywood, and she'd fallen asleep on her bed.

She sat upright and wiped the line of dribble from her mouth. "Come in."

Her dad poked his head in and offered her a giant grin. "I thought it'd be nice if you two met before everyone else."

Max felt as if she were about to meet the prime minister

and had forgotten to put clothes on. She wanted to warn her dad that it'd be better if the whole plan were aborted. She could already imagine the disappointment on her dad's wife's face as she took one look at the disheveled excuse for her husband's daughter.

But then she walked into the room.

Max tried hard not to stare and to keep her mouth from falling open. Her stepmother was tall with long dark hair and wore a pair of faded jeans and a T-shirt.

"Hello, Max. I'm Mee Lin. I am so excited to finally meet you."

She held out her hand. Max stared at her and said nothing. A few awkward moments passed where no one knew what to say. Finally her dad broke the silence.

"Ah, Max? Are you okay, honey?"

Her head jerked toward him and then back to Mee Lin. "What? Yes. Fine. I'm Max." She took Mee Lin's hand and shook it vigorously.

"L-Lovely to meet you," Mee Lin stammered as Max kept shaking.

"I think that'll be enough for now," her dad interrupted.

Max noticed she was still shaking Mee Lin's hand and instantly let go.

"We'll be leaving for the restaurant in about half an hour, but before we do that, Mee Lin has a present for you."

"It's just something small." Her voice was like silk. "I hope you like it."

*See Mission: Spy Force Revealed.

She held up a pink dress with embroidered flowers, a lace petticoat, and a matching bag. They were hideous. Max begged her face not to show it.

"It's great," she lied. "Really . . . great."

The only other time in her life she'd worn a pink dress was while working undercover during a Spy Force mission*, but then she'd had the excuse of saving the world. She tried to think positively. At least she wouldn't run into anyone she knew.

"We'll see you downstairs in half an hour?" Her dad kissed her on the forehead and they both turned to leave. Max smiled and waved, but when they'd gone, she slumped back onto her bed with the dress slouched across her lap like a piece of deflated fairy floss.

"Why couldn't I have acted like a normal person?" she said out loud.

"It's part of your charm." Linden appeared beside Max, and even though he'd just had a shower, his hair struggled not to look like the head of a toilet brush.

Max held up the dress. "Could this be any more ugly?"

"Only just, but look at it this way, you'll only have to wear it once," he said encouragingly. "Shame it has to be in one of the glamour capitals of the world."

Max put as much scowl on her face as it could handle.

"I'll see you downstairs." Linden figured now was a good time to leave Max alone, and left the room quickly.

Max looked at the dress. It was awful, but it wasn't the

dress that she was worried about. Mee Lin was beautiful and had the elegance of a princess. Max sighed. She'd happily wear pink for the rest of her life if it meant she could get through the night proving to Mee Lin she hadn't inherited the clumsiest stepdaughter in the history of the world.

CHAPTER 10

A High-Class
Restaurant and an
Unexpected Visitor

When they drove up the long, lamp-lit drive of the restaurant, which looked more like the rich home of someone very important, Eleanor leaned into Max and whispered, "We were told about this place. It's supposed to be one of *the* restaurants in LA."

"Great." Max slumped beside her aunt in her pink embroidered disaster.

Valets slid through the night air as if they were on Rollerblades, holding doors open, taking coats, and parking cars.

"Here we are," Max's dad announced. "This place has food that's a thrill ride for your taste buds. Who's in?"

Everyone eagerly stepped out of the car, except Max, who was busy trying to work out how to tell her dad she'd have more fun if she stayed where she was. Nothing came to her, so she dragged herself out and prepared to be as discreet as possible. She picked up the pink bag, which snugly held the Matter Transporter, and stuck close behind her dad, who, to Max's horror, was just about the most well-known person there.

"Hey, Bill, how's it going?"

"Bill, good to see you."

"Looking good, Bill."

Her dad smiled and said his hellos as Max did her best to become invisible. They wound their way between candlelit tables, around bubbling water features, and across a small wooden bridge over a gurgling stream.

"Very famous people often come here," Ben said quietly

in Max's ear. "If you're lucky you might see someone you recognize."

"Yeah, that'll be really lucky." Max slouched even more.

When they finally reached their table, Max leaped into a chair sheltered by an enormous palm. All she had to do now was hold off going to the toilet and hardly anyone else would see her.

After they'd ordered, Max's father launched into another one of his stories that had everyone laughing and wiping their eyes, and made Max momentarily forget her paranoia. Until she noticed Mee Lin staring at her.

"Max?"

Please can I say something intelligent, Max silently pleaded. "Mmmm?"

"Can I tell you a secret?" Mee Lin's voice was low and dangerous. This was the part where she told Max she was a loser and that the only way to explain Max's relationship with her father was that she was adopted.

"I was so nervous about meeting you today. I'd heard so much about you, and I worried that when you met me you'd be disappointed."

Disappointed? Nervous? Was she crazy?

"Your dad thinks you're perfect, and he's prouder of you than any dad I know." A warm smile spread over Mee Lin's face. "He's your biggest fan, and I'm afraid I've become one too."

Max blushed an immediate hot pink as her dad grabbed a glass and clanged his spoon against the side.

"I'd like to make a toast." Her dad loved giving speeches. "This is one of the happiest days of my life. I have two old friends with me, whom I've waited far too long to see. I've met Linden, who I'm told is one of the finest young men I'll ever meet—and that must be true because he laughs at all my jokes—and I'm with Mee Lin, one of the kindest, gentlest, most talented people I know." Max saw her dad look at Mee Lin and soften.

"But that's not the best part. I'm one of the luckiest fathers in the world to have Max in my life. From the day you were born, I couldn't imagine ever loving anyone more. You'll always be the most important person in my life."

"To Max," Ben chimed in.

Max shrank into her seat. She loved her dad, but why, like Ben, didn't he get that she hated having a fuss made over her? After the clinking of glasses had finished, her dad had something else to say. "Linden and Max, we need a few more extras in the film we're making, and I was wondering if you'd like to help out."

Max had just taken a bite of her bread roll. "Wou won uh woo aa in a wilm?"

Her dad frowned.

"Let me help," Linden offered. "You want us to act in a film?"

"Yep."

Max finished the rest of her mouthful. "That'd be . . . I'd love . . . if you think . . ." She tried to control her mouth but was failing miserably.

"I think that means we're in," Linden translated.

Three waiters appeared beside them and began serving their food.

"Your dad was right," Linden said to Max after his first bite. "This puts a whole new spin on the word 'taste.'" But just as he finished speaking, Linden thought he saw something strange.

"Max?"

"Mmmm?" Max was concentrating on the lobster claw that was slipping around in her hands.

"I know this is going to sound weird, but I think there's someone here you know."

Max's eyes followed Linden's finger as he pointed to a large fish tank and the wavering features of someone standing behind it. At first she thought it was just some kid with a fixation for teasing fish, until her brain kicked in and told her otherwise.

"No. It can't be." Her hands involuntarily squeezed the lobster claw so hard that it flew from her fingers and landed in the soup of a man sitting at the next table. He looked at Max accusingly.

"Sorry," she said as she winced.

An immediate bustle of activity arose around them as Max's dad and Ben apologized to the man and waiters instantly appeared to clean up the mess.

Max looked back at the watery kid who was sniggering as Linden tried to come up with an explanation for what they were seeing. "Maybe you're just facing one of your fears."

Max wanted to believe that, but the wobbling figure behind the fish tank motioned her over. "Wait until I get my hands on him," she simmered.

"It's your friend from Hollingdale, isn't it?" Linden asked.

Max's head ricocheted toward him. "He's not my friend."

But Linden was right. As the others were settling down after the soup incident, the wavering figure of Toby Jennings poked his smirking face around the tank. Max desperately struggled to stay calm.

She stood up and grabbed her bag. "I have to go to the bathroom," she announced a little more loudly than she'd intended. "Can you come with me, Linden?"

Her dad looked at her with concern. "Are you okay, honey?"

"Yeah. Fine. Great. Linden?"

Linden reluctantly lowered his fork to his plate, worried that he'd never see his dinner again. The pink lace of Max's dress swung vigorously behind her as she made her way to the fish tank.

"What are you doing here?" she asked menacingly as her hands flew to her hips.

Toby's eyes ran up and down Max's outfit. "Don't you think we should ask the big questions first, like what are you doing dressed like a raspberry marshmallow?"

Max's head filled with images of Toby being carried away by a giant snow eagle and dropped off the nearest snow-covered mountain.

"I'm here visiting you," he said.

"You just happened to be in Hollywood, in the same restaurant as me?"

"Actually, I went to your dad's house first, and after I explained I was a friend of yours, the housekeeper told you were here." Toby had an arrogant grin that Max wanted to wipe from his face and flush down the nearest toilet, but Linden was worried about something else. "How did you get here?"

"That's the best part." Toby paused for maximum effect. "I used Max's Time and Space Machine."

Max's mouth dropped open. Linden leaned across and closed it so she could tell him it wasn't true. Max rifled through her bag. "That's impossible because . . ." She saw the block of wood where the Matter Transporter should have been. "How . . . ?"

"Is that your dad?" Toby asked as if he hadn't just ruined her life.

Max couldn't answer. Her head was too busy with her new reality kicking out the old one.

"I'd like to meet him." And off Toby strode before Max or Linden could stop him.

By the time they made their feet work, Toby had reached the table and was already introducing himself.

"What are the chances of that?" Max's dad was delighted that she had run into a friend. "How long have you two known each other?"

"It feels like all my life," Max sneered, wishing her world was still Toby-free.

"I'm here with my parents on vacation," Toby lied.

"What a coincidence." Then Max's dad had an idea. "Max and Linden are going to be extras in a film I'm directing. Would you like to join them?"

This was turning out way better than Toby had hoped. Not only had he traveled halfway round the world using a machine that, only a few days before, he hadn't known existed, he was standing in the middle of a posh restaurant in Hollywood being asked to be in a film. The best part, though, was the look of horror on Max's face.

"That is, if it's all right with your parents."

"They'll love it." Toby smiled angelically. "They're always encouraging me to have new experiences."

Max watched the whole thing as if it were some twisted nightmare. Her life usually could be divided into two categories: the times when Toby was in her life and therefore making everything a misery, and the times when he wasn't. This was supposed to be one of the times when he wasn't.

"Great!" Max's dad beamed as if he'd just granted his daughter's most long-standing wish. "Here's my card. Get your parents to call me if they have any questions." Max's dad reached for a notebook. "Tell us where you are staying and we'll pick you up."

"No!" Linden and Max said a little too forcefully.

Ben and Eleanor frowned at their peculiar behavior.

"His parents can drop him off at the studio."

Now it was Max's dad's turn to frown.

"Okay. Done. We'll see you outside the studio gates at seven a.m."

CHEMIST

CHAPTER 11

Action!

When Max's dad said studio, what he really meant was a mini-city with streets, parks, shops, and giant hangar-type buildings where all the filming took place. The streets bulged with cars, film sets, couriers, security guards, and all manner of people rushing around in all sorts of outfits.

"Watch out, Max." Linden pulled her out of the path of a small open car as it zoomed past with important-looking people. This was followed by a slow-moving stretch limousine and a guy on a bicycle.

Max brushed herself down. "Thanks, Linden."

"Gotta watch the roads here," her father warned them. "Just because people are famous doesn't mean they know how to drive."

"Does it always take this many people to make a film?" she asked.

"Sometimes more," her father said as he led the way past a newspaper stand and a pretzel cart. "Ours is actually one of the smaller productions here at the moment."

"Does Steven Spielberg work here?" Toby spoke up from behind.

"Sometimes."

After they'd left him at the restaurant the night before, Toby had used the Matter Transporter to arrive in Max's room. Knowing she couldn't send him home because her dad was expecting him the next day, she begrudgingly let him camp on her floor. Far, far away from her bed. Early in the morning he left, and despite Max's hoping he'd end up in the outer regions of Mongolia, he met them in front of the studio gates at exactly seven a.m.

Her father's film set was like a giant warehouse that had no end. Lights hung from thick steel rods that disappeared against the blackened ceilings. Backdrops as tall as buildings with paintings of towns, mountains, and deserts were being wheeled around on carts that made it seem the world was moving. Sound swirled from all directions. Max felt as if she'd been dropped into some underground world where everyone went about their business like ants, each completing their own job with precision and pace.

After her dad introduced them to a few crew members, Max, Toby, and Linden met another man.

"And this," her father said, putting his arm around a pudgy, short man with superlong sideburns, "is Raychik. One of the best editors in the business and one of the best lasagna makers I know."

Raychik let out a wheezy cough.

"Nice to meet you," Linden said, even though he wasn't so sure.

Raychik offered them a grunt and hoisted up his drooping trousers before walking off into the darkened recesses of the studio.

"I bet the last time that guy smiled was when he had wind as a baby," Linden joked.

"Don't worry about him," Max's dad reassured them. "He is one of the nicest people in the business."

"If he's one of the *nicest*," Toby scoffed, "I think the dictionary's got a lot of explaining to do."

Max could feel her body tense when her dad laughed at Toby's joke.

Her dad moved away and started talking to a woman with a clipboard.

"Listen, sponge brain," Max snarled at Toby. "You're only here because I have no other choice now that you've invited yourself into my dad's film. If I had my way, you'd be sitting on the farthest side of the galaxy dodging asteroids. While you're here, don't talk to me, don't get in my way, and"—she added with particular force—"don't tell my dad any more of your stupid jokes."

"Don't worry, Max, I'll make sure your dad likes you better than me."

Max fumed, partly because Toby was being mouthy but mostly because he'd guessed exactly what she was thinking. His being near her physically was bad enough, but she definitely didn't want him going anywhere near her brain.

"As if my dad would like you better than me." She laughed, trying to sound convincing. "Just stay out of my way and don't do anything that's going to attract attention."

Max turned and walked straight into a clothes cart. She clung to the fluff and sequins on the costumes as the cart began a nonstop collision course through the studio.

"Max!" Linden ran after his friend and tried to stop her, but it was too late: Max and her runaway cart ran smack into a ladder that started to sway like a tree that had just been sawn through.

"Timber!" joked Toby.

The ladder came crashing down, leaving the guy at the top swinging from the thick black curtain he'd been repairing. Crew members flew into action to save him, but the curtain started to tear, and the whole thing ripped like a ship's sail in a storm. He landed in a black cushioned heap beside Max, and even though she knew it wouldn't do any good, she said it anyway. "Sorry."

It was then she noticed the entire crew had stopped what they were doing and were staring at her. At times like this Max wondered if she was too young to volunteer for an extended stay on the international space station.

"Okay, everyone," the woman with the clipboard announced into a microphone. "Filming starts in twenty minutes."

Instantly everyone went back to work.

"You okay?" Max's dad asked her.

Apart from wanting to trade herself in for a kid who wasn't a complete disaster, "Sure," she answered quietly.

"Good. Carla will take care of you and show you what you're going to wear."

A woman with a hair wrap and a long colorful gown led them into a darkened corridor to the wardrobe department. She handed them each an outfit. Max took the frilly dress with the bustle and feathered hat and knew that, after the damage she'd done, she had no room for complaint. "Thanks, Carla."

They were to be three rich kids from the late 1800s in New York. Toby and Linden got into their suits and laughed as they tried to out-posh each other.

"As impossible as it may seem," Toby whispered, "that dress suits you even more than your pink one."

Max ignored him as she sat before a well-lit mirror and the last of her makeup was applied. A voice yelled into the room, "Places, everyone."

Suddenly actors and extras came from everywhere and spilled onto the staging area. Max lifted her skirt and stared at the studio, which had been transformed into an early morning in 1876. It was amazing. As if she'd been transported straight into . . .

"Ouch!" A man in a dark suit knocked her in the head with his cane and walked off without noticing.

"These were rough times. Especially for women," Toby said knowledgeably as he polished his hat with his gloved hand.

"They'll be especially rough for you if you don't stay away from me," she warned.

"Action!"

The scene bustled to life as hundreds of extras milled around her. Cameras moved along tracks while others swung over their heads on cranes. After a few minutes of this, Max's dad called, "Cut!"

It was then arranged that more specific movements would be filmed. A man with a baseball cap and a tragic mustache called to Max and Toby.

"I want you, little girl, to stand beside this shop. And you,"—he looked at Toby—"when I give you the nod, you sneak up and kiss her."

Max fumed at a few things: being called "little girl," the idea that Toby had to kiss her, and lastly, the fact that Linden thought it was so hilarious. She was about to protest when everybody was told to take their places and "Action!" was called again. Max stood by the shop window. The guy then nodded and Toby did as he was told, only when he went to kiss Max, she was so repulsed she pushed him away and he fell through the shop window. There were screams as actors sprang back from the fallen pane.

"Medics!"

People from the first-aid area raced over and checked Toby out. They fussed over him and asked him questions to make sure he was okay. The glass had fallen out in one solid piece, and apart from a red mark that was developing on his cheek where Max had hit him, he was fine.

"Does your boyfriend know what happens when you're kissed?" Toby rubbed his cheek and looked toward Linden.

"He's not my boyfriend," Max replied.

"Ah, Max?"

It was her dad. She'd been in California for only a day,

and she'd already managed to prove to him that she was an oafish, useless, muddleheaded, dim-witted idiot. As Max lifted her long skirt and dragged herself over to her father, she felt the crew's scowls circling her like a pack of hungry vultures.

"Maybe you and your friends should have a break and get something to eat from the canteen." Her dad suggested with a gentle smile.

The woman with the clipboard screamed, "Ten-minute break till we fix the window."

The three young actors made their way outside as Toby and Linden talked about the window stunt.

"That was pretty impressive," Linden said. "I thought you'd be cactus after a fall like that."

"I do judo. You learn how to fall without hurting yourself."

As the two new friends talked about stunts and favorite films, Max slumped along behind them, while from out of the darkened wings, a blackened figure stared at her. He watched Max's every move as a small cough escaped from his broad, wheezy chest.

CHAPTER 12

A Chilly
Invitation and a
Surprise Mission

Although she was nervous, Max surprised herself and most of the crew by finishing the rest of the day's shoot without breaking anything—or anyone.

"Where are we going now?" Toby asked excitedly.

"I'm going home with my dad, while you can—"

"Good work, kids." Max's dad walked up to them. "Toby, you want a lift?"

Before he could answer, Max butted in. "He was on his way to meet his parents."

Linden thought he saw Toby's smile slip.

"We'll see you for the shoot in three days then, eh!" said Max's dad.

They said good-bye to Toby and walked to the car, where they sank exhausted into the leather seats.

"This film business is hard work," Linden said, and sighed as the driver maneuvered the car onto the busy LA streets.

"Linden, Max, I have a surprise for you."

"A surprise?" Max sat forward.

"How about a ski trip to Aspen?"

"I'm in," Linden offered.

"But your work . . . ," Max began.

"That can wait. My little girl's visiting." Max's dad handed her a brochure of a snow-covered chalet-style hotel. "This is where we'll be staying. You used to love skiing when you were little."

Back in Max's bedroom, Max and Linden flopped onto the bed just as Toby did another appearing act. "This is the best trip I've ever been on. I never knew hanging out with you could be so much fun, Max." He saw the ski brochure. "Are we going skiing? I love skiing, and this hotel looks great."

That was it. Toby had been getting on Max's nerves ever since he'd first arrived in LA, but now she'd had enough. "I think you've forgotten, this is *my* family reunion and *my* life, and even though you've found yourself in the middle of it, it has nothing to do with you."

"Oh, Max." Toby put on a hangdog look that had "faker" written all over it. "And there I was thinking our relationship was finally starting to blossom."

Max narrowed her eyes and got ready to let him have it, as Linden peeled a banana he'd picked up from a fruit bowl, and settled in to enjoy the show.

"What I'd like to know is who said you could make your home on my planet?" attacked Max.

Toby's smile spread across his face like warm honey. That was more like it. "Scientists call it commingling of the species. Lesser life forms learn from more intelligent ones, which means you've still got a lot to learn."

Linden took another bite of his banana and swung his head back toward Max as if he were at a tennis match.

"And to think your mother went through all the pain of childbirth just for you."

"At least when I was born my mother had something to celebrate." Toby grinned.

"Maybe her tears of joy were really tears of despair." Max smiled wickedly, but Toby wasn't beaten.

"At least they had no trouble telling I was a boy."

Linden smiled and turned again to Max. For an instant he thought he saw her falter, but she came back more strongly than ever. "Did it take you long to have that thought, or did you have it shipped in specially?"

"It popped into my brain. That's a small gray organ you may not be familiar with."

"I know what a—" but Max's response was interrupted by a knock at the door.

"Max, open up. It's Ben and Eleanor."

Ben and Eleanor! They couldn't know about Toby, at least not until Max had worked out an explanation for how he'd appeared there. "Coming," she shouted in a slightly too-sweet voice as she shoved Toby toward the wardrobe. "Get in there," she grumbled.

"You really don't take losing very well," Toby struggled to say as he was being forced into a pile of white, fluffy bathrobes and spare blankets.

"In case you've forgotten, no one knows you're in

here," Max answered. Then she added forcefully, "And I didn't lose."

She slammed the wardrobe door before giving the nod to Linden to let her uncle and aunt in.

"Were we interrupting something?" Eleanor inquired as she stepped gingerly into the room.

"Nothing I can't tell you about later," Linden joked as Max shot him a prickly glare. "I mean, no."

Eleanor wasn't convinced. She passed a quick eye over the room before making her way to the couch and taking out her palm computer.

"How was your day?" asked Max, doing a terrible job of trying to appear normal.

"Interesting," said Ben as Eleanor logged on. "We met with Harrison to show him the new Time and Space Machine, but we were interrupted by Steinberger, who had some disturbing news about a mission."

"A mission?" Max perked up at the word.

"And lucky for us, it's here in Hollywood."

"Where's Harrison now?" Max asked, keen to see the head of Spy Force again.

"He returned to London to organize the logistics of the plan," Ben explained.

Steinberger appeared on the screen of the palm computer. "Max, Linden. How good to see you again and how lucky you're there. Here at Spy Force we've uncovered a fiendish plot within the film industry, and we'd like you two to head the mission to stop it. In fact, with Ben and Eleanor there to offer backup, we couldn't think of a better team for the job."

Linden shot Max a sideways smile she quickly returned.

"We're not sure of all the details yet and will be in touch in a few days to tell you more," Steinberger continued. "We do know that someone within the movie industry is using the studios for evil means, and we need you to find out as much as you can about how the movie business works and who the big movers and shakers are. Which isn't a bad job. I love the movies. Why I even—"

Suddenly Steinberger seemed to be gasping for air.

"Steinberger? What's wrong?" Eleanor watched as the agent grabbed his chest and tried to suck in great clumps of air. "Steinberger?"

She was about to contact other Spy Force personnel to help the ailing agent when the reason for his discomfort appeared on the screen.

"Hello, Steinberger."

It was Frond, the head of the Plantorium at Spy Force. Using only plants for her ingredients, she could make any potion, from invisibility cream to anti-sag buttocks lotion, and was the only known cause of breathlessness in Steinberger, apart from a good bout of jogging.

"I got here as soon as I could." She noticed the palm

computer and pushed her rose-shaped glasses along her nose. "Oh, you've made contact already. Hello, everyone."

"Hello, Frond," breathed Eleanor, relieved that Steinberger's heart wasn't giving out on him after all. At least not in the way she'd thought.

Unable to speak, Steinberger stared at Frond as her long, red lab coat swirled beside him and her hair rose above him like a miniature Tower of Pisa.

Ben whispered to Linden, "Hasn't he told Frond how he feels about her yet?"

"Not yet." He shrugged.

Ben's eyes widened. "We used to take bets on when he was going to tell her. Looks like I lost by about five years."

"We'll get started right away," Max told a breathless Steinberger.

"Bye, everyone," Frond answered.

Eleanor shut down the palm computer.

"What should we do about Aspen?" Max asked.

"Your dad told me about that. It's very important that we do nothing that seems unusual," Eleanor instructed. "Which means going skiing as planned. While you're there, listen out for anything about the industry that may give you clues as to what is happening."

"What should we do first?" Linden moved to the edge of the couch, excited about the idea of another mission.

"The pact," Ben said decisively.

"The what?" Max asked incredulously.

"The pact," Ben repeated. "You know, where we all hold—"

"Hands. I know." Max sighed.

"Linden told us how you do it before every mission," Eleanor added.

"Did he?"

Linden smiled broadly as he took Max's hand and one by one they each swore to look out for one another always.

A sound from the wardrobe sent Eleanor's head turning in that direction. Max's brain was alive with a million excuses she could use to get out of the questions that were about to flow, but all Eleanor asked was, "How's Toby?"

Max frowned. "Sorry?"

"Toby? Your friend from school?"

"Good." Max had been ready for almost any question except that one.

"Good," said Eleanor, but Max could tell she knew more than she was letting on.

"Have a great trip, and we'll see you when you get back." Eleanor kissed them good-bye, and Ben gave both their heads a rub before they left Max's bedroom.

When the door closed, Toby leaped out of the wardrobe wearing a long, oversized robe. "A mission? How great will that be?"

"It's for us, not you," Max said abruptly.

"You know, anyone would think you didn't like me, Max Remy."

"Would they now?" she fumed.

"Yeah. Lucky we know otherwise."

He noticed a piece of fluff on his gown. "Hey, Max, I think you've dropped your brain."

"Why don't you—"

"Oh, Max?"

It was Eleanor. Max booted Toby under the bed with a firm shove just as the door swung open and Eleanor walked in.

"I also wanted to—"

"Yes?" Max asked a little too eagerly.

Eleanor stopped. "I wanted to let you know Quimby is getting a mission pack ready for you both for when you return from the ski slopes."

Quimby was the Spy Force inventor who equipped spies with special devices for each mission.

"Excellent. Quimby's great, isn't she? Always one step ahead." Max knew she was rambling but found it hard to stop. "Spy Force sure is lucky to have her. In fact, I don't know what they would do if—"

"We'll be ready to start the mission the moment we get back," Linden said, stepping in.

A moment passed.

"There's nothing going on that we need to know about, is there?" Eleanor asked.

Linden thought fast. "From what Steinberger told us, I think there probably is. We'll do our best to find out all we can while we're away." He looked earnestly at Eleanor as Max sat on the bed, her lips glued together for fear of what might come out.

"Right." Eleanor turned and narrowly missed stepping on Toby's hand as she left.

Max locked the door. Toby stood up and brushed himself down. "Boy, that was close. You were nearly caught that time. You need to be more careful."

"Me be careful? It's your fault I'm in trouble in the first place. If you hadn't stolen the Matter Transporter . . ." Max was so angry she hardly knew what to say first.

Until it came to her.

"I want you to go home. We're about to go on a serious mission, and we can't afford to have anything or anyone mucking it up."

"Are you serious, and miss all this fun?" Toby laughed again.

"I mean it," Max said pointedly.

Toby eyed her with a determined stare. "But what about your dad? He'll get suspicious if I don't show up for filming."

"I'll tell him you're busy. And besides, what about your parents? Won't they be worried?"

"Doubt it."

"Why's that?" Linden was curious.

"Because they're in Austria."

Max was stumped. "Austria?"

"They're heart specialists and were asked to go there to help with research." Toby shrugged. "It's no big deal. I live with Aunt Mable, who's eighty and lets me do whatever I want. She thinks I'm staying with friends."

Linden stared. "Don't you miss them?"

"My parents?" Toby pulled his robe around him. "They'll be back."

"What about school?"

Toby grinned. "Aunt Mable's eyesight isn't great without her glasses, so a note'll be no problem."

Max felt bad about Toby's parents just leaving him like that, but if she let him be part of the mission, she could be kicked out of Spy Force.

"You still have to go."

Toby paused. "No."

This was as good a standoff as Linden had ever seen. It was the gunfight at the OK Corral, the lion eyeing off the gladiator, the crew about to mutiny on the *Bounty*.

Max had to get Toby out of there. "Don't you think you've caused us enough trouble already? Then again, that's all you are, Toby Jennings. Trouble. From the moment I met you you've been nothing but a major nightmare to me, and the only way my life is going to be anything other than miserable is if you disappear from it completely."

Toby looked hurt. "You really mean it?" he asked softly.

"Yeah, I mean it," she said, not so forcefully this time.

"Okay." Toby dropped his bathrobe to the floor and

made his way to the middle of the room. "See you, Linden. It was fun hanging out with you," he said sadly before turning to Max. "Bye, Max. I'll give you this when you get home." He held the Matter Transporter toward her. "I never meant to cause you any trouble."

He entered the coordinates into the Matter Transporter.

"Give me back the . . ." Max demanded. But it was too late. With a small *fffftt* and a flash of green light he was gone.

"I'd better get ready for dinner." Linden left the room quietly, leaving Max standing in a pool of guilt that was deep enough to dive into. She tried to step out of it by telling herself it was wrong of Toby to steal the Matter Transporter and it was against the rules for him to be involved in a mission.

It didn't help.

What she'd said was true. She did want Toby out of her life. So why, after she got what she wanted, did she feel so terrible?

CHAPTER 13

An Unwelcome
Reappearance and a
High-Speed Snow Chase

She'd done it. Max Remy had captured one of the most fiendish villains the world had ever known. On the surface he was all charm, but inside was the heart of a pure criminal. She'd scoured the world to find him, and now his unlawful days were over.

"So, Baron Von Jenkins, what do you have to say for yourself?"

The baron adjusted his monocle and straightened his gold-embroidered waistcoat as the wind outside his ancient castle headquarters blew softly against them.

"That I'm innocent and have been set up."

Max laughed as she snapped a pair of handcuffs around Von Jenkins's wrists. "Set up? Come on, now. You're one of the most evilly cunning people in the world, how would you let yourself be set up?"

"You laugh now, Ms. Remy, but even the most clever of us sometimes find we haven't been clever enough."

This was unlike Von Jenkins. Max felt herself starting to believe him and was furious that he would try to fool her. It had taken her a long time to track down his hideout, and she wasn't about to let him get away now.

"I've had enough talk." She placed a chain around his ankles and waited for the Invisible Jet to arrive that would transport them both to Spy Force HQ. "I suggest you enjoy your last moments of freedom, because when we're done with you, you'll be going to prison for a very long time."

"Wait!"

Max turned to see agent Linden Franklin climbing the rocky cliff behind her.

"We were wrong. The baron was set up. He's really a good guy."

Max balked. Could this be true? Could the baron really be innocent? She stared at his cool stance as a sinister smile rose up his face. Had she really let herself be duped? Was she

The plane jolted in the air. Max grabbed the armrest so tightly she expected there'd be finger indentations if she ever decided to let go. Her father reached over, slowly pried her fingers away, and held her hand.

"Look out there." He nodded at the window next to Max. "It's beautiful, isn't it?"

Outside were snow-covered mountains jumbled together like giant tenpins in some freakishly big bowling alley. The sun sluiced over the landscape in a blinding glow as the plane dipped its wings and began a wide sweeping arc toward the runway.

"This part might be a bit bumpy, but the guy at the front's been flying these planes longer than you've been alive."

Max's dad had the kind of voice that made you feel

calm. That people paid attention to. At the studio his directions were always given in a relaxed, gentle way, and everyone listened and did what he said.

Max smiled and looked at Linden, who was staring out his window and chatting with Mee Lin. She thought back to the night before. She felt bad about what had happened with Toby, and even though Linden hadn't said anything, she could tell he thought she'd overdone it.

After a few more bumpy turns and silent mini–freak-outs from Max, the plane touched down. They stepped onto the tarmac, and the cold wind hit their faces as if they'd been slapped with frozen towels. Max pulled her jacket around her as they made their way to a swish car.

"How many of these cars does your dad have?" Linden asked as they stepped into a warm interior the size of a small living room.

"Not sure," Max answered, happy that Linden was still talking to her.

The car made its way up a snaking mountain pass, past snow-filled trees and frozen waterfalls. A white blanket of powdered snow covered everything, and when they reached their hotel, there were cozy fireplaces, thick fluffy rugs, and as many hot chocolates as they could drink. Their rooms were the size of a small street, and when Max pulled aside her curtain, the shiny white slope of one of the tenpins swooped in front of her like her own private ski run.

"Mee Lin has something for you both," Max's dad

announced. Mee Lin handed two sets of snow clothes to Linden and Max.

"I hope you like them."

Linden held out aqua blue pants with a white stripe on the side and a straight-cut jacket with a waving white stripe across his chest. Subtle, stylish, and very wearable.

"Excellent. Thanks, Mee Lin."

Max's, on the other hand, was a giant pink snowsuit with cream swirls.

"I know how much you liked the dress, so I thought I'd buy you this," Mee Lin said happily, as if she'd handed Max the keys to a secret underground chocolate supply.

"Thanks. It's really . . . unique," Max barely managed.

"You two get settled in and we'll meet you in the foyer in ten minutes for a ski."

Max stared at the suit, then noticed Linden slowly creeping toward the door.

"Go on," Max dared him.

"What?" he asked innocently.

"Say something about the suit."

"Sorry?" Linden was running low on "innocent-looking."

"The suit? What do you think?"

He pulled the collar of his sweater away from his neck. "Is it warm in here or—"

"Linden."

He couldn't ignore the warning oozing out of that one word. Linden had no choice. He couldn't lie, she'd pick that up right away, and he couldn't tell her the truth, because even if he'd been dropped on his head at birth, he'd never be that stupid. He decided. There was nothing more to do . . . other than beg.

"Please don't make me say anything. There are too many things I've planned to do when I'm older."

Max sighed and sank onto her bed. "At least I won't run into anyone I know here." Then she needed to ask something else. "Linden, do you think I was wrong to ask Toby to leave?"

Linden stopped. "I think you said what you needed to say."

Max gave him a half smile. It was true, but she still didn't feel any better.

But then something happened that made her guilt disappear completely. There was a green flash of light and a familiar, quiet *ffftttt* sound.

"Did your dad pick the swankiest hotel or what?" Toby stood before them in a blue snow jacket and matching pants.

Max was furious. Not only because his suit looked better than hers, but she now realized Toby had never had any intention of staying away.

"I went home to say hello to Aunt Mable. This Matter Transporter is great. You can travel the world and still pop home for lunch."

"Don't get too used to it." Max was annoyed that she'd

wasted good quality guilt on him, and strode into the bathroom.

"This is better than I expected." Toby surveyed the room, opening fridges and wardrobes, and checking out the TV Guide.

Max came out dressed in her snowsuit. "One word," she warned. "Not one word."

The boys were quiet. Even Toby knew not to comment. "I think I might try all the restaurants to see which one has the best hot chocolates." He pulled his beanie down low and quickly made his exit.

Max hadn't been skiing for a while but despite being the clumsiest person alive, she was actually quite good. Her fury at Toby melted away as she and her dad raced down slopes of fresh powdered snow. Mee Lin had been skiing since she was a kid, and Linden, who had never been on a snowboard in his life, made it look as if he'd been born standing on one.

At the top of the mountain Max and her dad decided to try different runs. "Meet you at the bottom," her dad cried before skiing away.

"Okay." Max turned and, making her way through a crowd of skiers, slammed into the padded bulk of a man.

"Sorry," she apologized, before realizing it was Raychik. "Oh, hi."

He coughed and grumbled something about needing to be here, before he disappeared into a swarm of beginner skiers as they wobbled and fell and got tangled in their poles.

"What's he doing here?" Max queried out loud.

She shook off the weird vibe the unexpected meeting had given her and made her way to the top of the ski run. She started thinking about Toby and how it must have been hard to have both parents live away from him, when her thoughts were cut short by what happened next.

A skier shot out from the bushes in front of her, only narrowly avoiding clipping her skis. "Hey," she yelled, but the skier didn't stop or signal and instead swooped across the snow and aimed directly at her. Max tried to ski faster, but soon the skier was beside her and shot Max a malicious grin before ramming into her. She regained her balance but not her direction, and careened straight into the forest.

Max maneuvered her skis around mounds of rocks and smaller trees, each one a potential silent killer. She could see another run beyond the trees and knew she only had to go a little farther to reach it, but her skis landed badly on a jagged outcrop and flung Max into the air, causing her to come crashing down with a dull, painful thud.

The next thing she remembered was someone leaning over her, asking if she was okay. She opened her eyes and let out a brief gasp. It was Raychik.

"I saw someone skiing recklessly just after we bumped into each other." He wheezed and coughed. "There are always cowboys on the mountain showing off."

Max tried to work out where she was.

"I used to be a ski patroller when I was younger,"

Raychik explained as he checked her over. "You'll be a bit sore tomorrow, but nothing's broken."

Max was groggy and her eyes felt weighed down by steel. The next time she opened them, she was in the medical center with her dad standing over her.

"Max? Can you hear me?"

After she was given the all clear by the medical staff and way too much fuss by her dad and Mee Lin, Max was taken to the hotel and cushioned up in front of the fire.

"Lucky Raychik was there when he was." Her father smiled at her in relief. "He's right. There are always fools on the mountain trying to prove they're invincible." He kissed her forehead and left her with Linden while he went to get them something to eat.

"So, what's your next trick? Diving from a plane with no parachute?" Linden tried to cheer her up.

Max looked around, making sure the other guests couldn't hear. "The skier who ran into me did it deliberately."

"Maybe they didn't like your suit," he joked, but Max's steely gaze let Linden know she was serious.

"You really think they wanted to kill you?"

"No. They could have done that easily. I think they wanted to scare me."

Linden lowered his voice. "Who do you think it could be?"

"I don't know, but I don't think it was an accident that Raychik was so handy."

"Do you think it's about the Spy Force mission?"

"Not sure, but that skier was upset about something." Max trembled as she thought about how close she'd come to being really hurt, and knew that next time she might not get off so lightly.

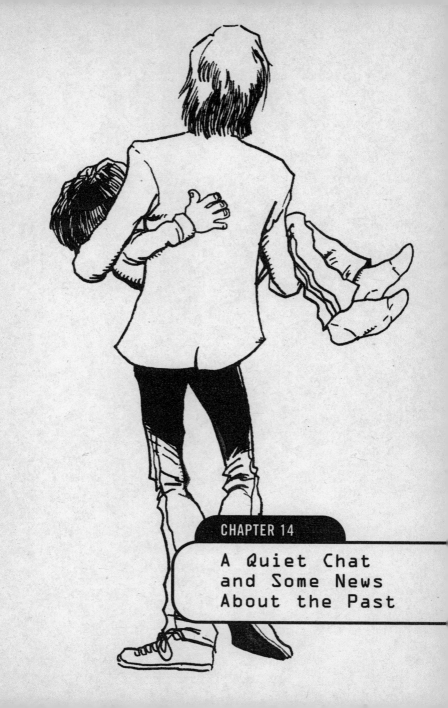

CHAPTER 14

A Quiet Chat
and Some News
About the Past

When Max woke up, the first thing she saw was her father's wide smile.

"Hello. You've been missed."

It took her a moment to remember where she was. And to remember the fall. She went to move but flinched with pain.

Her dad's smile dropped, and he quickly put down the papers he was working on. "The doctor said you might be a bit sore, but that shouldn't last too long."

The fire had died down yet still threw out a strong orange glow.

"You scared me today. Promise me there'll be no more accidents."

"Okay," Max agreed, and remembered the mission Steinberger had given them. She needed to gather information about how the film industry worked, so she asked her dad about who held the power, who made the decisions, and who had direct contact in creating the finished product. Her dad explained that it was different for each film, but mostly the producers, editors, and directors had the biggest control.

Max ran through the information in her head. Since the director of her father's movie was her dad, she knew the bad guy wasn't him. She'd find out about the producer when she got back to Hollywood, and after meeting the editor, Raychik, she planned to keep a close eye on him.

"I never knew you were so interested in the film business."

Max looked up and saw her dad smiling. She felt another twinge of guilt. She'd never been very interested in what her dad did, and now she was only asking because of Spy Force. "Do you like what you do?"

Her dad got this wistful look in his eyes. "It's like breathing, Max. I couldn't imagine what I'd do if someone told me I couldn't make films anymore. It was a big decision when I first thought about moving to California. I knew it'd be great for my career, but I also knew it would put a lot of pressure on your mom and me."

So their divorce wasn't all her mom's fault, Max thought.

Her dad sighed. "Remember you and your mom and I used to go skiing all the time when you were younger? You were only three when you had your first skiing lesson, and the moment you got on that snow, you were a natural. There was a coach there who wanted to sign you up for the Olympic ski team there and then."

Apart from never having been called a natural at anything before, Max smiled as her head filled with memories of snow fights, hot chocolates, and falling asleep in front of fires as her mom and dad laughed and talked into the night. She wanted to ask what went wrong, when her dad spoke up and answered her secret thoughts.

"Your mom and I began to want different things," he

said sadly. "I still think she's one of the nicest people I've met, but when you stop bringing out the best in each other, you're not being fair to anyone by staying together." Max's dad looked at her intently. "Even though we don't live together anymore, you and I will always be the same. You know that, don't you, Max?"

Max felt as if her body were covered in bubbling waves. It was true. Being with her dad again, it felt like nothing had changed between them, but Max wanted to tell him that she still missed him saying good night before she fell asleep. Waking up each morning knowing he wasn't in the house was something she'd never gotten used to.

"How's your mom? Is she okay?"

"She's okay," Max began. "She's getting married."

"She told me," her dad said carefully. "Is he a good guy? Because you and I have to make sure he is good enough for her."

Max wished her mother could hear what her dad was saying and how important it was to him that Aidan was okay.

"He's all right," she lied.

"Good."

They sat in silence for a few minutes before her dad said, "Time for bed. After the day you've had, you're going to need all the rest you can get."

He gently picked her up from the couch to carry her to bed, and even though with all her bruises it should have hurt, she snuggled into his neck and didn't feel a thing.

CHAPTER 15

An Angry Outburst
and a Secret Plot
Revealed

It had been a rough day and the soreness from Max's fall was starting to ache, but it wasn't the bruising that had caused her the most pain.

They were back in Hollywood, and Max, Linden, and, of course, Toby were extras again. Her dad was having a bad day. She'd overheard a few of the crew talking about the film running over budget and the leading actor threatening to walk off the film, and the way her dad was acting, he wasn't happy about it either.

The woman with the clipboard spoke into her microphone. "Okay, let's go, people. We have a film to make and a deadline to keep."

Max was worrying about the change in her dad's mood when Toby came up to her, biting into a bread stick. "Your dad looks a little stressed."

"He's not stressed." Max was so used to disagreeing with everything Toby said, she contradicted him automatically. He was right, though. Her dad did look stressed, only she wasn't going to admit it to Toby.

Max stayed out of her father's way all day, but when it came to going home, he hardly even noticed she was there.

"Mmmm? Oh, Max. You and your friends go home with the driver. Mee Lin's away for a few days filming in San Francisco, but there's plenty to eat in the fridge. I'll be home late." Then he added, "I'm going to be busy over the next few days so I won't be able to spend much time with you."

Toby looked at Linden, who shrugged. This wasn't the Max's dad they knew.

He turned away and started talking to a member of the crew. Max's shoulders slumped as she walked to the exit of the studio. She could hear voices behind her becoming heated and turned to see her dad arguing and throwing his hands around.

Linden, Toby, and Max walked through the studio grounds to the car in silence. Linden knew Max was sad, and he wanted to cheer her up. "He's had a rough day."

"Or maybe he's sick of me already?"

Linden frowned. "How could anyone get sick of you?"

"Well, first of all—" Toby began, until Linden elbowed him in the ribs.

"Maybe he wishes he'd never had me."

"Max, he'd never wish that." Linden leaned into her gloomy face and shone her one of his best smiles. "When you meet great people, you never regret it."

Max smiled back. "One of your mom's sayings?"

"Yep. I've been saving that one for a special occasion," he replied proudly.

Toby frowned. He wasn't sure who was acting stranger, Max's dad or these two.

"And Mee Lin never mentioned anything about going away."

"Maybe it came up unexpectedly," Linden suggested.

"Or maybe she's over me too?"

At her dad's home all three collapsed on the couch in exhaustion.

Until there was a knock at the front door.

Max sat up, jumpy from the day she'd had at the studio and her attack in the snow. She looked through the curtains and shuddered when she saw a man in a uniform carrying two parcels. The last time she'd received a parcel it had almost led to the destruction of spy agencies across the world.*

"What if it's the man who tried to kill me on the slopes," she whispered.

"A killer who knocks?" Linden questioned.

"Killers can have manners too, you know," Toby reminded him sarcastically.

Max ignored them and grabbed one of her ski poles that had been left in the hall.

"You don't think there's a possibility it could be someone else?" Linden asked.

"Who else could it be?"

As Linden thought of the many other people it could be, there was another knock.

"Coming." Max ushered Toby and Linden to the other side of the door.

She again looked through the curtain and saw something that made her heart go cold. The guy's delivery uniform was too small for him, and beneath it Max could see a different layer of clothing. The real delivery guy was probably lying in the garden somewhere while this phony had taken his suit, put it on over his clothes, and was here to kill her.

Max clenched her teeth and flung open the door. Before the guy could say anything, she hit him with her pole. He fell to the ground with a pained groan and a thud like a sack of potatoes.

"Max?" Linden and Toby leaped out from behind the door to see the crumpled figure of the guy beside two parcels.

"What did you do that for?" Toby asked, worried Max's skiing accident had dented her brain.

"He's not a real delivery person," she said with more than a hint of victory in her voice. "These aren't his real clothes."

"I've heard better reasons for whacking someone," Toby mumbled.

The guy put a hand to his head and let out a moan.

"Who are you?" Max stood over him with the ski pole held above him.

"My name's Brad." The guy rubbed his sore head.

"Prove it," Max ordered.

"It says so on my name badge."

"He's right." Toby read the guy's badge.

"The badge would have been on the suit when he stole it. Check his wallet," Max instructed.

Linden looked at the guy. "Do you mind?"

The guy shrugged. Linden pulled his wallet out of his pocket and read the name on the license. "It is Brad, actually."

Max frowned. "Let me see that."

She stared at the photo of the guy on the doorstep and the name Bradley Walker. "I thought you were . . . I was only trying to . . . I've been a little jumpy since . . ."

"Can I help you up?" Linden offered the guy his hand.

"I think I might do it myself," said Brad as he pulled himself up. "If you could just sign this form, I'll leave you alone."

Max took Brad's pen and signed. "I'm really sorry, I . . ." But Brad had turned and was on his way down the driveway.

Linden turned to Max. "Max, promise me something, will you?"

"What?" she asked contritely.

"Make it a rule to find out who people are before you attack them."

"Okay," she promised, feeling guilty for about the millionth time that week.

Seconds later there was another knock on the door. Max grabbed the ski pole as Linden jumped in front of her. "Why don't I see who it is this time?" He looked out the window. "It's Ben and Eleanor. Maybe it'd be better if you disappeared, Toby. They'll want to talk about the mission."

"You can hide in my room," Max offered, and he quietly slipped upstairs.

"Why do you think he likes hanging around so much?" asked Linden. He couldn't help thinking it wasn't just the mission Toby wanted to be involved in.

"Beats me," Max answered. "I wish he'd find someone else to be a shadow for."

Linden opened the door. Ben and Eleanor swooped in with their usual hugs and kisses. "Are you two okay? We were worried sick. Was there any more trouble?"

"No. Nothing," Max replied into the layers of her aunt's clothes.

Ben spied a bowl of fruit on the hall table and picked out an apple. "How was your form, Linden?" Ben knew about Linden's ability to pick things up quickly.

Linden shrugged. "All right, I guess."

"I knew it," Ben mumbled through a mouthful of apple. "You got it on the first try."

"Oh!" Eleanor exclaimed. "You've received your Spy Force parcels. Those delivery people are very efficient."

"And lucky to be alive," Linden said out of the corner of his mouth. He looked at Max, worried that one day her temper would get them into serious trouble.

Before Ben could ask what he meant, Eleanor's palm computer lit up.

"Steinberger," she announced. "Bring your parcels to your room. It'll be safer to talk to him there."

Max and Linden shot each other a quick look that Eleanor spotted. "Is there something wrong?"

"Of course not. Why would anything be wrong? Everything's fine. Completely fine," Max rambled.

Eleanor wasn't so sure as she and Ben climbed the stairs with a nervous Max and Linden following closely behind, but when they walked into Max's room, everything seemed normal. Max scanned the room carefully, poking her head into the bathroom and checking the wardrobe, but found no Toby.

"Are you okay?" Eleanor queried.

"It's just the fall," Linden explained, giving Max a *Calm down* look. "She's been a bit funny ever since it happened."

Ben ran the Securicore over everything, checking for bugs and looking for any signs of tampering, while Eleanor took a small metal globe from her pocket. As she lifted it into the air, it lit up like a sparkler and she drew a wide sweeping arc that left a glowing green curve around them.

"What's that?" Linden was impressed by the flickering dome shape.

"A Shush Zone," Eleanor explained as she logged on to Steinberger. "It creates a restrictive sound field that stops anything we say from leaving this area."

"No bugs, Steinby." Ben dropped his apple core in a wastebasket as Eleanor prepared to take notes.

"Excellent. Glad to see you all again. And Max, I'm sorry to hear about your fall, but I, like Eleanor, think that it was no accident."

Max trembled at the memory. Linden saw her worried face and gave her a nudge—one he hoped reminded her of their pact to look out for each other.

"In your parcels you'll find all you need for your mission. Your pack doubles as a Personal Flying Device, and I know how much you loved the PFD on the last mission, Max."

Max groaned. Using the PFD hadn't come very naturally to her.

"Inside each pack is a Danger Meter, which, as you know from your first mission, is to be worn beneath your clothes and vibrates when danger is close. You'll also find a flashlight, a knife, a laser, and a pair of heat-sensitive X-ray glasses. Not only will they find concealed objects, but they can pinpoint the location of a human in dark or hidden places by emitting a red pulsing glow. Finally, there's one of Plomb's dustless, soundless bombs and detonators. You, of course, have your palm computers with the built-in locator, and other equipment will be given to you by a secret contact we have specially placed in the studio since the attack on Max."

He went on to explain the mission. "An eminent scientist has been kidnapped. He was working on a part-time basis for Spy Force. He never was a man to sit still too long, so he worked for us whenever he was in the country."

"He's an adventurer?" asked Max.

"No, he's one of the world's most accomplished walking champions. He's won medals for it in almost every country. Not for me, all that hip swinging and feet to the floor at all times. In my younger day I could have—"

"What do we know about the kidnap?" Max interrupted before they were all forced to take a trip down Steinberger's crowded memory lane.

"We know he was kidnapped because his home was left in a mess. He is a meticulous man who breaks into a sweat if anything is untidy for even a few minutes. There was an unmade bed, and eggs that had been boiling on the stove long enough to make them bounce when they were thrown against the wall."

"How do you know that?" asked Linden.

"One of the agents tried it out."

Max and Linden were curious why the agents had nothing better to do in the face of a kidnapping than throw eggs around, until Steinberger continued.

"They did this to estimate the time the eggs had been cooking and hence how long our scientist had been gone. Estimated kidnap time was three hours fifteen minutes and forty seconds earlier. We knew then that Dr. Fartie was in trouble."

Because they were in the middle of a mission briefing, Ben and Linden did all they could not to laugh at Dr. Fartie's unusual name.

"We're not sure who kidnapped Biggus or what they plan to do with him, but we think it has something to do with the work on encoding he was doing for us. Or it could be his study of methane gas emissions, we're not positive yet."

Linden sat on his hands and Ben squeezed his lips between his teeth. A laugh as full as a belly after Christmas was trying to wiggle its way out of each of them.

Linden wanted to make sure he had things straight. "So, Dr. Biggus Fartie was working on smelly gases?"

"That and encoding," Steinberger answered seriously.

Eleanor let loose a small smile before concentrating even more intently on her notes. Max was annoyed at how much Ben and Linden were starting to fidget.

"Whatever the plan, we believe Fartie's kidnapping can only mean one thing," Steinberger added dramatically. "That someone, somewhere is carrying out a plot that has the stench of something rotten about it."

Linden squirmed and Ben let out a muffled snigger. If there was any more talk of farts and smells, they were going to lose control completely.

"Biggus Fartie is one of our best scientists. I want you to sniff him out, find out what evil he is being used for, and save him before another foul-smelling plan is let loose on the world." Steinberger wished them luck and signed off.

That was it. Ben and Linden let loose. Even Eleanor joined in.

"What?" Max cried as they collapsed in laughter around her.

Ben tried to explain as his cheeks ballooned in and out with fits of guffawing.

Linden and Eleanor collapsed into each other as clutches of laughter shook their bodies. Max stared at them and wondered if she'd been zapped into another dimension, one where nothing made sense. Linden fell off his chair and didn't even seem to notice.

Max thought she'd give them time to control themselves. "I'll get some things to eat while we discuss our game plan."

"Max!" Eleanor called out, but she was too late. A resounding *clunk* rang out as Max bumped into the Shush Zone.

"Ouch!"

"Sorry." Eleanor deactivated the device as she tried to stifle a few stray giggles. Max glared at them as she rubbed her head, wondering what it would take to be on a mission with serious agents, and for her not to be so clumsy.

CHAPTER 16

A Maritime Disaster and an Ominous Warning

"Max. Hold on!"

The squalling wind acted on the lake like a blender, tearing into the air in a frenzy, ripping through trees, and biting into Max's face in a searing sting.

Max and her dad were on assignment in Finland, a country Max loved, with its lakes as big as oceans, and calm, tree-lined landscapes. The day had been perfect, washed over with blue skies and the gentle whir of nature, until Dr. Ruma Hakinnan detected their presence and activated his weather machine. He planned to use the machine to demand vast sums of money. If he was refused, the world would face imminent meteorological disaster.

Hakinnan sent a savage storm exploding across the lake. Max lost her balance and was hurtled over the side of the boat. Her dad flung his hand out and caught her just in time.

"Hold on," Max's father called out again, but she was losing her grip. The rain and the churning lake lashed her face, and she swallowed huge gulps of water that filled her lungs. The force of the wind and the thrashing of the waves made it hard for her dad to pull her into the boat. A huge wave swelled behind them.

"Look out!" Max watched in horror as the boat tipped and threw her dad into the swirling waters.

"Dad!" Max grabbed on to the boat's edge as she tried to see her father. His red life jacket was no more useful than a raincoat as the waves heaved over him. What was she going to do? Her father was being dragged away from the boat. If she let go, they'd both be lost. She had to think of a plan to save him. To stop him from being dragged under

"Aaaaahhhh!" Max sat up in bed as water wormed down her face. She gasped for air and threw her arms around as if she were drowning, desperate not to die.

That is, until she saw Toby standing over her with a glass of water.

"I never knew you were of such great value." Toby continued laughing.

"I told him not to do it, but he wouldn't listen," Linden said in his own defense.

"What are you doing here?" She turned into her pillow, hoping they'd go away.

"Max, when are you going to realize I just can't live without you?" Toby's sarcasm was about as welcome as a bucket of spiders. "Plus, we were supposed to meet your dad in the hall five minutes ago for today's shoot."

Her head spun round to the clock. It was 6:35. She'd slept through her alarm. Why was it that on every other boring day of her life the slightest sound woke her, and when she had something important to do she slept in?

"You better take your PFD and put your Danger Meter on. We may need it," Linden advised.

"PFD?" Toby remembered reading about them in Max's diary. "Are they really flying backpacks?" His eyebrows shot up his forehead at the thought of trying one, but Max was too busy getting dressed, attaching her Danger Meter, and worrying about how upset her dad would be. She patted down her hair and grabbed her pack, and they all ran downstairs.

"Max, I have a film to shoot, so when I ask you to turn up on time, I mean it."

Max felt the sting of her father's words against her face as if she'd fallen headfirst into a beehive. He'd never spoken to her so abruptly before, plus he'd broken his own rule that no matter how annoyed he was he would never tell her off in front of other people.

As her dad walked to the car, Toby watched Linden offer Max a warm smile. Her face transformed from completely miserable to almost happy. Linden could do that with Max, Toby noticed, as if he knew a secret route straight into her thoughts.

They were silent the whole way to the studio as Max's dad read through his notes.

"This is Mimi." Max's dad introduced them to a young woman wearing a headset and carrying a pile of papers. "She's looking after the extras today." And with that he moved into a swarm of people buzzing with questions and holding out more notes.

They followed Mimi through the chaos and noise of cast, crew, technicians, props, clothes stands, and backdrops. Max turned to catch a final glimpse of her dad, but he'd disappeared amongst it all.

"I like what you've done with your hair, Linden." Mimi kept up a firm pace.

Linden had no idea what she was talking about. "Sorry?"

"It's the earthquake scene today, and that hair of yours sure is playing the part."

Linden smiled proudly. "Yeah. It's a natural."

Mimi led them to the wardrobe department, where they took off their packs and were fitted out with old clothes that looked as if they'd been dragged through a swamp.

"You're going to play three street kids caught up in an earthquake. No one cares about you, and you are very much left on your own when the quake hits."

The way she felt, Max wouldn't have to do much acting as she plunged her hands into her baggy, patch-ridden overalls.

"Shall I take your packs?" Mimi asked.

"No!" Max said, a little too forcefully. "I mean, no, we'll keep them with us."

Linden and Toby stood side by side in their short pants, suspenders, and torn shirts.

"You're going to be fighting off the girls in that," Linden said with a smirk.

"I don't need clothes to impress girls. It's all about what's inside." Toby grinned.

"What? Hot air?" Max asked.

"No. Charm. Something you might learn about if you watch closely."

Mimi then led them to their next destination, a place that made Linden's broad smile wash across his lips.

"I'm in heaven." His mouth sagged opened as his eyes swam through a pleasure zone of pastries, bagels, rolls, boxes of cereal, yogurt, fruit, and steaming trays of eggs, sausages, and bacon.

"Have something to eat. Filming starts in an hour. I'll come for you then."

Toby and Linden began piling food onto their plates and found themselves a seat at a long table full of other breakfast eaters. Max sat with them, picking at a bowl of muesli as she watched her dad bark orders and yell demands.

"If I'd known you were fed so well on film shoots, I'd have taken up acting years ago," Linden mumbled through a mouthful of scrambled eggs.

"Max, you and I definitely have to do this more often." Toby crunched into his second hash brown smothered in ketchup.

Max heard none of it as she watched her dad throw a clipboard across the room and storm off with Raychik following closely after him. Something wasn't right about her dad, she could feel it, but she didn't know what. She stood up to take her plate across to the wash area, when she heard something familiar.

"Pssst."

She looked around her and saw the usual clutter and bustle of crew.

"Pssst."

"Agent 31?" She adjusted her backpack and tried to work out where the secret agent was concealed. There were trays of muffins, boxes of bread, and huge bowls of fruit.

"Pssst."

Max frowned. "Even 31 couldn't get into there." She walked over to the table nearby and looked down into a giant toaster.

"Hi, Max. Great to see you again."

"Agent 31? But how . . . ?"

"Good, huh? I can tell you're impressed. It was tricky getting in, but after a few twists and turns, I did it. Watch out, here comes some whole wheat."

Max stood aside as a guy with a piece of whole wheat bread stuck it into the toaster. She smiled as they both waited for the bread to cook. After a few awkward moments he took his toast and walked away. Max again leaned into the toaster.

"What information do you have for us?"

"It's even more involved than we thought, and

Harrison has dispatched a few agents into strategic positions to find out what's going on. We have firm proof that Fartie was kidnapped because of his work with encoding and believe he is being forced to program hidden secrets into films bound for worldwide distribution."

"Who do you think is behind it?"

"We're still working on that, but it seems Raychik is somehow involved, and a silent producer we're currently trying to identify."

"Max, are you going to use the toaster all day or . . ." Linden held out two bagels and smiled. "Agent 31! This has got to be your best yet."

"It's up there, but I still don't think it's as good as the wallet I snuck into on the French ambassador back in '92."

"You hid in someone's wallet?"

"Not just anyone's. The ambassador's."

Linden and 31 had this way of completely forgetting they were on a mission.

"Are we done reminiscing?" Max asked.

"Sure." Linden tried to look serious. "What have I missed?"

Agent 31 filled him in before adding, "We'd like you and Max to gain access to the edit room and check out the editing process."

"Does that mean we have to talk to Wheeze-man?" Max complained.

"Raychik," Linden explained to 31's puzzled stare.

"I'm afraid it does, but we'll have agents in position so that if anything funny happens, they'll spring into action immediately."

Max felt better. This place was really starting to make her nervous.

"In your pockets you'll find miniature digital cameras especially designed by Quimby. Shockproof, waterproof, and detection proof."

"Yeah, but are they Max-proof?" Linden smiled before his face collapsed into a pained expression. "Tell me I didn't say that out loud."

"You'll keep," Max replied. "Go on, 31."

"Once you're in the edit suite and have distracted Raychik, place the cameras in positions that will give us a good view of what he does. Ben and Eleanor will be positioned in the back of a surveillance van in the alley behind Studio 23 monitoring everything. Contact them as soon as the cameras are in place."

"Anything else?" Max examined her thumbnail-size camera.

"Yeah," Agent 31 said with an extra level of seriousness in his voice. "Try the boysenberry jam. You won't regret it."

"Thanks, 31." Linden headed off toward the jams, as if their meeting were really about food and not saving the world.

Max's head was full of ways to get into the edit suite as

she made her way back to the table to find Mimi ready to usher them into their positions.

"You can leave your bags here while we shoot. They'll be safe, I promise," she said to Max's wary gaze.

Suddenly extras came from everywhere and were being given directions as Max's dad spoke to the lead actor and actress. Max was determined not to muck anything up as she, Linden, and Toby prepared to act.

Panic and chaos filled the studio as the floor below them rocked into life.

"Earthquake!"

Cameras swung on cranes above their heads, while others were pushed alongside them on tracks. Lights flared from every angle, and crew members stood behind her father taking notes, holding boom mikes, and standing ready with makeup cases.

Toby and Linden seemed to be enjoying every moment of the fake quake, falling and stumbling through broken glass and crumbling debris and bodies.

"Hey, watch out!" The chaos swallowed Max like a freak wave, knocking her to the ground. After what felt like hours and some pretty hefty shoving and stampeding, her dad called, "Cut!" The chaos stopped, and Max looked up from the floor as a giant centipede of legs walked back to where they'd come from.

She wiped a sprawl of dust from her face. "At least that part's over."

"Stand by for another take," a loudspeaker voice called.

"Another one?" Max groaned. "I only just made it through the first one."

"First positions, everyone."

A hand appeared in front of Max's face. "I didn't know this Hollywood business was so much fun." Max looked up expecting to see Linden but saw Toby instead. Toby only ever offered Max anything in preparation for doing something mean. "You were great. Really convincing." He'd been watching her? And was giving her compliments? Maybe she'd hit her head harder than she thought when she fell.

"We'd better get ready. They're about to start." Max got to her feet without his help.

"Oh, yeah."

They made their way back to their first positions, and after a few people threaded through the actors checking their hair, makeup, and wardrobe, the scene began again.

"Action!"

Max went into earthquake mode and did exactly as she was instructed, but then she caught sight of Toby and realized she was experiencing a weird feeling she'd never felt before. What was it? It wasn't quite like she was going to be sick, but it was similar. Why now? Maybe it was to do with her dad. Or maybe . . . and at this point she really felt sick . . . maybe it had something to do with what Linden had told her when he came to her school. Maybe Toby did like her. A disoriented policeman trampled her as she tried to take this thought in. How could he like her when he'd made her life a misery from the first day they'd met?

"Cut! That's it for the extras for now. Meet back here in half an hour."

Max looked up from the muddied curb she'd fallen into and spied Linden. She jumped up and raced over to him.

"Let's get out of here before Toby sees us."

"Sorry?"

"I mean, so we can get to the edit room."

"Oh, yeah. Good idea."

After grabbing their packs, Max and Linden made their way out of the studio and along the snaking corridors to the edit room.

"Here goes," she said as she stood in front of the door and knocked.

They heard nothing.

"Do we just go in?"

"I guess." Max turned the handle and entered the dimly lit room to see Raychik huddled over the edit suite. Her body tensed as she remembered seeing him after her fall on the ski slopes, and realized she could be looking at a man who was out to get her.

Linden stepped forward. "Raychik?"

The editor spun round in his chair and eyed the two

kids warily. "What do you want?" he mumbled irritably, turning back to his controls.

"We're interested in the editing process and were wondering if we could watch what you do?" Linden asked, hoping Raychik wouldn't throw them out.

Raychik grunted as he continued his work. "Whatever."

Linden found a seat beside him. Max stealthily took out her camera and stuck it in the foliage of a sagging plant before sitting down and winking at Linden.

Raychik worked as if they weren't there. Linden had to somehow put his camera in front of the editor to get a different angle from Max's. He looked at her, signaling for her to create a distraction. Max took the cue and threw her arms back into a big stretch, knocking a pile of film canisters to the floor.

Raychik groaned.

"Sorry. I didn't mean to . . ."

Linden took his chance to position his camera as Max and Raychik picked up the canisters and placed them back on the bench. But as Raychik turned back, he saw Linden sit down quickly. The editor paused. Seconds ground past like train wheels skidding on a metal track, eating into Max's and Linden's nerves.

Then he went back to work.

They were in the clear. Or so they thought.

"I know what you're thinking."

The sound of those few words made them stop breathing.

"But watch out," Raychik cautioned threateningly. "The film business can be a dangerous game."

Max and Linden looked at each other, not knowing what to do.

"Now you'd better get out of here before you're wanted on the set."

They didn't need to be told again, but as Max and Linden hurried out of the edit room and down the corridor, Max felt her Danger Meter vibrate. Behind them two men in suits moved quietly out of the shadows. They stopped and stared at the two disappearing spies before turning and entering the room.

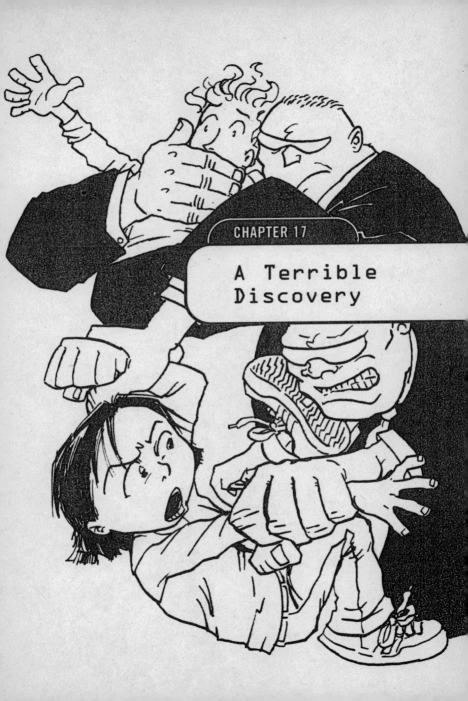

CHAPTER 17

A Terrible
Discovery

Later that day Ben and Eleanor called Max on her palm computer. Once the cameras were in place, it hadn't taken long for them to make an important discovery. Soon Max and Linden were on their way to the van behind Studio 23 to find out what it was going on.

As they walked along the busy studio streets, dodging minitrains of cancan dancers, workmen pushing giant brooms, and a tour of overweight businessmen, Linden guessed the reason for Max's mood. "It must be really stressful making a film. I bet that's what's up with your dad."

"Yeah, but I've never seen him like this before," Max said miserably. "It doesn't feel like him."

"You haven't seen him for a long time."

"I know, but he wasn't like this at the slopes."

"Maybe when he's working it gets a bit much sometimes."

"I know my dad, all right?" Max wasn't sure what was making her angrier, what Linden was saying or that her dad really had changed since she'd last seen him. She felt bad about snapping at Linden. She'd never let anyone say anything against her dad, but something more was upsetting her.

"It just feels sometimes that neither of my parents wants me. Or has time for me."

Linden started to say that wasn't true, but Max cut in, "And Toby thinks I'm ugly."

Linden frowned. "How do you know Toby thinks you're ugly?"

"He said so before, in my room. You were there. You heard him."

Linden struggled to remember. Max let out a sigh. "He said when I was born, they couldn't tell whether I was a boy or a girl."

Linden scrabbled through his brain for the part in that sentence where Toby said she was ugly. He decided to avoid what he didn't understand and go with what he knew. His mother always said it was best that way.

"Max, I think you look good."

"You're just saying that because you're my friend. Toby thinks I'm ugly, and he said it right out loud in front of everyone."

"In front of me," Linden reminded her, wondering if they were talking about the same conversation.

"I am ugly. Even my mom says I have a plain face."

Linden thought about what to say next and worded it as carefully as he could.

"Max, I think your mother and Toby are so far wrong that they need to go in for emergency eye-testing as soon as they can."

Even though it was the last thing she felt like doing, Max laughed. Linden could do that. Things could be bleak and he'd say one thing and everything would be fine again.

"And while they were there, I'd book them in for a personality installation as well."

But then he could also say things that went too far. Linden's smile faltered as Max's face went so red it could have been used as a warning beacon in a blizzard. She tried to do something to make things less embarrassing. She looked at her hands, twisted the end of her hair, stared at the sky, and still only seconds passed.

Finally, to Max's relief, they reached the truck.

After knocking, a hidden scanner above them discreetly revealed who they were to Ben and Eleanor, who opened the door and ushered them in with hugs and kisses.

"Well done." Eleanor beamed. "Those cameras are in excellent positions."

"Just doing our job." Linden sighed importantly as they both sat down.

"And we've finally had a chance to show Harrison the Transporter Mark II—via the palm computer, of course, which does minimize the impact." Ben pulled the device from a small leather bag next to him. "He thinks it's the most amazing invention he's ever seen."

Max was impatient to get back to their mission. "What have you found out?"

Eleanor shot Ben a quick look before beginning. "An ultrasensitive heat ray within our monitors has picked up an unusual device in the edit suite that appears to alter the film. It's the size of a small beetle and is markedly similar to

Fartie's encoding device. We've sent the information to Quimby, who is almost certain it is one of Fartie's."

"So they *are* trying to hide messages in films?" Linden asked.

"It seems," Eleanor replied, but there was something in her voice that told Max she wasn't telling them everything.

"What else did you find out?" Max asked guardedly.

Eleanor sighed as she rewound the tape. "Now Max, it might look bad, but there's probably a perfectly reasonable explanation."

A knot tightened in Max's stomach as Ben pressed the play button to reveal Raychik sitting at his desk working. Two men dressed in suits walked in and asked the editor if he'd done what he'd been told. Raychik calmly replied that he wouldn't at any price. It was then that Max's dad walked in and started yelling at the editor. He was screaming abuse and threats. Finally, he told Raychik he was fired.

The editor stared at him. "We've worked together for years. We've always been able to work out our differences."

"Well, maybe you're more trouble than you're worth and it's time I got rid of you."

Max saw the pained expression on Raychik's face. "If that's what you want . . ."

"Yeah, that's what I want," Max's dad said coldly.

The editor stood up to leave. "I don't know you anymore."

"Maybe you never did."

Raychik put his hands in his pockets, gave one last look at Max's dad, and left.

"Maybe that's what Raychik meant when he said the film business could be dangerous," Linden deduced. He turned to Max but realized she wasn't thinking about Raychik.

"I'm sorry, Max." Eleanor put her hand on Max's shoulder, but she pulled away.

"That doesn't prove anything against my dad," she said confidently. "Except that he doesn't want to work with a grumpy editor."

Eleanor gave Ben a quick look before she turned to her computer. "We need to find out who is behind the encoding and which films have been tampered with. Hopefully we'll find our answers before any highly sensitive material is dispersed."

"You've done well," Ben said to Max and Linden. "I'm so proud I—"

"We've got to get going." Max cut him off.

"Max," Eleanor said, but Max ignored her and strode out of the truck. Linden gave Eleanor a clipped smile before quickly following.

"They think Dad's involved. I know it," she said when he'd caught up.

Linden was silent.

"The footage showed nothing," she fumed.

Linden was still quiet.

"You saw that, didn't you?" She turned on her heel and faced Linden, who looked away. Then she realized. "You believe it too, don't you? You think my dad's a criminal?"

"But the footage . . . ?"

"My dad would never do anything like this."

She ran off quickly, ducking into a narrow alley.

"Max!" Linden shouted after her, but she wouldn't listen as she flung away tears threatening to worm down her face. Her father was a good man. How could Linden think he was bad?

Just then a van pulled up and blocked the alley. "Hey, I'm trying to get past."

Max's Danger Meter began vibrating, but she was too upset to notice.

The van stayed where it was. She slammed her fists into the back windows as the doors were flung open and two men jumped out.

"I said, you're in my way," she seethed as her hands flew to her hips.

"Max!" Linden entered the alley just as the guys were forcing Max into the van. He ran at the guys and tried to beat them off, but they were too strong, and within seconds he and Max were lying in the van, gagged and bound, unable to move or scream for help.

"Drive at normal speed," one of the goons ordered the driver. "We don't want no one getting suspicious."

As the van pulled slowly out of the alley, a disheveled figure emerged from the shadows and, keeping out of sight, followed the vehicle to its final destination.

CHAPTER 18

A Bad Mood and
a Deathly Fall

"Does the zoo know you've escaped, because I think you should tell them in case they get worried," Max spat at her captors as she wriggled in the ropes that tied her to an upright wooden stretching rack. Her Danger Meter vibrated silently beneath her clothes.

The two goons had taken the young spies to a torture chamber lined with iron manacles, whips, and cruel-looking devices for twisting and imprisoning. A stony balcony circled the top of the chamber, looking down on several rocky levels. The only door in the chamber was set into the wall of the balcony and led to a set of roughly chiseled stairs that descended to the bottom level. In the center of this was a large round pit.

Max's stretching rack was positioned on the balcony and from there she had a full view of the chamber and the pit. The goons stood rigidly by the door, as if they were awaiting further orders.

"You know, I've had more interesting discussions with plants than with you."

Max spied their backpacks lying on the lower level of the chamber. The goons had thrown them aside thinking they were normal packs.

Linden was imprisoned in a cruel-looking contraption on a platform above the pit. His wrists and ankles were gripped by manacles that held him inside a coffin-shaped metal cage that had doors lined with spikes. Linden did all he could to stay still to avoid the sharpened points. He'd been quiet until now, but he could see Max's taunts were starting to get to the goons.

"Ah, Max. Maybe getting these guys upset isn't such a good plan." He felt the regular vibration of his Danger Meter under his shirt.

Max kept on at the goons. "What's wrong? Have you put your brain somewhere and you're trying to remember where?"

One of the men flinched and sent her a gnarled stare. Linden knew Max was upset about her dad, but there was something reckless about the way she was acting. "Max?"

She looked down at him. "I haven't decided I ever want to speak to you again yet."

She turned away.

Linden tried to make her understand. "I know you're angry with me, and I bet you're right about your dad. I bet he isn't involved in anything. I want to help you prove it."

Max clenched her teeth, determined not to be talked out of her mood. Suddenly her Danger Meter vibrated even harder.

"Linden, you're always playing the good guy, aren't you?"

Max and Linden looked toward the man who was walking down the stairs.

"Dad! You're here! I knew you'd come. These guys kidnapped us and are working for someone who is using the studio to transmit top-secret information throughout the world." Max was so happy to see him. Then she realized he wasn't rushing to free them.

"Dad?" Her voice was small and unsure.

Linden's hair prickled on his head and stood even higher than usual. The way Max's dad was looking at them, setting them free wasn't what he had in mind.

"So, you've gotten yourself into a bit of trouble?" He reached the bottom of the stairs and walked toward Linden. He touched the sharpened end of one of the spikes. "Maybe it's because you were sticking your noses in where they didn't belong."

"But, Dad. I know you don't mean that," Max said quietly from above.

"Oh, I mean it. You think you know me, but it's been a long time since you and I have lived together, and quite a few things have changed."

"But you said that you and I will always be the same." Max tried to reconcile her father of a few days ago with the one she was talking to now.

"Did I?" He rubbed his hand across his chin in mock confusion.

Linden eyed Max's father carefully. He remembered Max telling him what her father had said. Why was he denying it now?

"I must have forgotten. Come on, Max. You're a clever girl. You know sometimes we say things because they're the right things to say, not because we believe them."

An aching wave shot through Max's chest.

"I mean, really. It takes very special people to like each other for a long period of time, and I don't think you and I are that special."

This hurt the most. This was one thing he'd always said to her—they were special, and nothing would ever change that. Max's eyes sank to stare at her shoes.

"Are the distribution trucks in place?"

Max looked up, her eyes blurred with tears, and realized he was speaking to the goons. "Why are you talking to them? They're part of the plan to . . ."

Then her dad did something that snatched the breath from her lungs. He placed his hand under his chin and, taking hold of the skin, tore a latex mask from his head.

"Blue!"

The man below her slowly ran his hand through his blue-streaked hair. "Yes. Lovely, isn't it, that we're all together again?"

Max's mind unscrambled itself as she began to understand what had happened.

"So, you're behind this whole encoding business?" Linden accused him.

"I rather like to describe myself as being a supporter of the arts."

"You're the silent producer!" Linden glared coldly.

"Yes, but most people know me as Albert Power. Suits me, don't you think?"

Max shivered with anger. "What have you done with my father?"

"Maxine, if I tell you everything now, this is going to be a very quick visit, and I do so look forward to our meetings."

She fixed Blue with a venomous gaze. "If you touch him or hurt him in any way, you'll regret this day for the rest of your life."

Blue took her gaze and answered it with a syrupy smile dripping with victory. "Max, I'm quaking in my cowhide boots."

Linden pushed against his manacles, furious at the way his friend was being treated. Blue was baiting her, and the mood Max was in, she might just snap.

"Anyway, with what's going to happen next I think you should be much more worried about your own future rather than that of a man you rarely see."

"You shut up about my father!"

Blue sighed. "Your loyalty to a man who hasn't bothered to visit you in over three years is astounding."

"He's been busy. Besides, he's done lots of things to let me know he cares."

"Like walking out on you?"

Linden flinched. The vibrations of his Danger Meter hammered against his chest. Blue was playing a very dangerous game.

"He didn't walk out on me." Max's voice was low and hard. "He left to work in Hollywood."

"And be with his new wife and child," Blue added.

"They don't have any children," Max spat back, but the way he smiled, she could tell Blue knew something she didn't.

"They didn't tell you Mee Lin is going to have a baby?"

An invisible cold lump slammed into Max's chest.

"I guess they didn't think you were important enough to tell. After all, once they have their own child, they won't be needing you anymore."

Max wanted Blue to stop talking. If her dad and Mee Lin were going to have a baby, he would have told her.

"Max." Linden looked up at her. "He's only trying to upset you."

"What would you know! You think my dad's a criminal, so don't pretend to defend him now, you hypocrite."

Linden recoiled from Max's words as they echoed around the chamber, bouncing off the rocky walls. Max's heart jolted at his saddened face. She was angry at Linden for thinking her dad was a criminal, but mostly she was angry because it might be true. "Linden, I—" she began, but Blue interrupted.

"Children, let's not fight." He was enjoying every moment of their arguing. "I need to tell you how my chamber works."

"But this isn't real," Linden reminded him. "We're in a film studio, remember?"

"Linden, that's where you're wrong. I had this place especially designed for your visit. It's based on an old torture chamber where spectators stood on the balcony eating roast goat and drinking brewed ale as they watched prisoners writhing in the pit below with snakes, spiders, and centipedes as their squirming companions."

Linden stared into the pit before him. "What are you going to do with the films?"

"Ah, that is so exciting I can hardly contain myself. The films are encoded with top-secret information that the United Nations would hate to be made public, such as all sorts of facts about international security. The messages are digitally encoded onto the film's surface like a layer of invisible ink that will make me lots of money and won't interfere with the audience's viewing of the film."

Blue's malevolent eyes were alive as he relished his role in the possible destabilization of the world.

"The UN has got a hard enough job trying to bring peace to the world, and you're going to wreck that?"

"Oh, Linden, there you go on your goody-goody crusade again. The UN are a bunch of old fogies dominated by a few countries working for their own benefit. You're smart enough to know that. It's time I benefited as well."

"What's in it for you?" Linden asked with contempt.

"Enough cash to furnish my rather expensive lifestyle and a bunch of other things, including a castle in Bavaria I have my eye on."

"Where's Fartie?"

Blue was starting to get annoyed at Linden's questions.

"You know about Fartie? He's somewhere safe. Now, if you don't mind, I have work to do."

Blue summoned his goons and began quietly talking to them.

He had to be stopped. If the films were distributed as planned, Linden knew the destruction they'd unleash would be devastating. He felt the corner of his palm computer against the fingers of his manacled hands. He ran through the keys in his mind. If he could get a message to Ben and Eleanor, they could use the locators in their palm computers to find Max and Linden before it was too late. That is, until what happened next.

"You'll never be half the man my dad is, Blue," Max said. "You're just a sniveling excuse for a man, who wouldn't know the first thing about loyalty or elegance."

There was something about the way Blue looked up at her that made Linden's blood freeze. *Please don't hurt her*, he pleaded silently.

"I've warned you before about pushing me too far." There was a barbed-wire edge to Blue's voice as his reddened eyes glowered at Max, but it wasn't her he headed for. It was Linden. "And now you'll see why. Release him."

One of the goons moved toward Linden. He pulled a lever that unlocked Linden's manacles and slowly tipped the iron cage toward the pit. Max stared in horror at what she was seeing, hoping it wasn't real, hoping it would stop. She breathed against the insistent pulsing of her Danger Meter.

Linden didn't say a word as he gripped the cold metal of an opened manacle. His legs flayed the air as the goons sniggered like mangy hyenas. "Maybe next time you'll learn when to stay quiet," Blue said maliciously, before turning and leaving the chamber.

Linden's grip slipped as the iron cage dangled him over the pit. One by one his fingers came away from the metal, until, silently, he fell through the air. In a soundless, desperate moment he caught Max's eye before he fell into the pit with a sickening thud.

"Linden?" Max stared at his crumpled body, which lay askew on the floor.

In her mind she saw the look of dread on his face as he fell again and again. She wanted to catch him, wanted to make it stop, but she couldn't, and all that was left was the twisted sprawl of her best friend's body as he lay in the darkened pit below her.

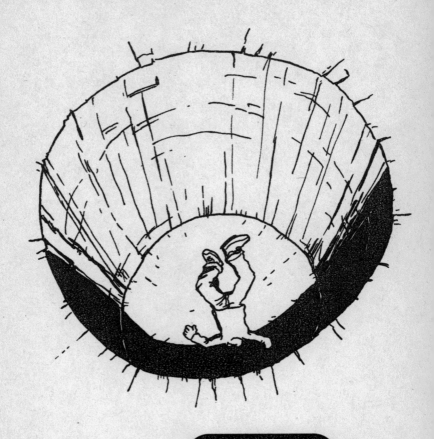

CHAPTER 19

A Mission Through Time

Max clenched her fists and pushed her arms against the ropes of the stretching rack. She felt as if she'd been dragged beneath the surf by a huge, thundering wave, dumped into a murky, swirling oblivion. Her hearing and sight were muffled and all around her was chaos.

Linden lay at the bottom of the pit. Unmoving.

Everything became still, as if time had stopped and left Max stranded in the eerie aftermath of Linden's fall. She couldn't tell what was the beating of her heart and what were the warning signals from her Danger Meter. She tried to block out the look on Linden's face as she'd watched helpless, unable to stop him from falling.

The sound of dripping echoed around the stone chamber.

"Linden?" It snuck out as a frightened whisper.

Nothing. He lay on the stone floor. Motionless.

They'd made a pact. Max knew Linden would have done anything to save her, and all she'd done was put his life in danger because she couldn't keep her temper under control. She turned away, tears clogging her eyes. "Please. I'm not sure who is listening right now, but I'll do anything to get Linden back. He's the only real friend I've ever had. Please don't let him be dead. I'll do anything if you'll help me save him. Anything."

"Anything?"

Max looked down to see the smiling face of Toby, who'd stepped out of the shadows from a secret entrance in the lower wall. "What are you doing on that . . . ," he began, but Max's shoulders shivered, and as much as he told himself he was wrong, Toby thought she was crying.

"Max?"

She didn't answer. Something wasn't right. Toby followed Max's gaze toward the gloomy darkness of the center of the chamber. It took a few moments for him to make sense of what he saw.

"Linden!"

Linden's face was pressed against the floor, and as Toby moved closer, he saw a small trickle of blood at the corner of his mouth.

"Is he . . . ?" Toby turned toward Max.

"He won't move." Then Max remembered something. "There are some heat-sensitive glasses in my pack. They locate life by emitting a red glow."

Toby ran to Max's bag and found the glasses. He gave her a hopeful look as he put them on and saw the red glow from her body. He stared down into the pit. His heart lurched, desperately hoping Linden was okay, but no matter how hard he looked, he couldn't see it. There was no red glow.

"Well?" Max was petrified of what he would say.

He took off the glasses and gave a small shake of his head.

Max began to quietly sob as Toby climbed the stairs and stood beside her. He felt as if he should put his arm around her or touch her shoulder or something, but he couldn't work out what. "What happened, Max?"

"This guy Blue was here with some goons and he . . . he . . ." She couldn't say it.

"I'm sorry." Toby's eyes itched with tears. He blinked to drive them away and to drive away what the glasses had shown him was true. He liked Linden. He was smart, had a great sense of humor, and wasn't scared of anyone. And now he was dead.

Max gasped back a choked sob. "I was so horrible to Linden just before he fell." Her words caught like burrs in her throat. She'd been so mean to him when all he'd ever been was a true friend. "I yelled at him and called him a hypocrite." Max saw herself shouting at Linden over and over again and was saddened by every second of what she'd done. "How could I have said that? Linden was the best friend I've ever had."

This time she couldn't hold back. She turned her head into her shoulder and wept.

Toby hated seeing Max like this. His heart twisted as he looked down at Linden and knew he had to do something— he couldn't let Linden die.

He put Max's glasses in one pocket, pulled a penknife from another, and cut through her ropes.

"I know what we're going to do," he said. "This new Time and Space Machine, does it really travel through time?"

Max nodded limply, like a doll whose batteries were

running low, not even wondering how Toby knew about the machine.

"How does the time bit work?"

She stared at him in disbelief, silent tears falling down her face. She didn't want to talk about the machine. She didn't want to talk about anything. "Linden was my best friend, and now he's . . . I've lost my best friend."

"I know," Toby replied carefully. "But there's somewhere we have to be."

Max's body was so heavy she couldn't imagine ever moving again.

"Max," Toby said with more force. "Tell me how the time part works."

Max gathered the last amount of strength she had and explained how to travel through time using the Transporter Mark II, including the part about being invisible.

"Where is it now?" Toby asked.

"With Ben and Eleanor."

"In the van at the back of Studio 23?"

"How did you . . . ?" Max was starting to wonder how Toby knew so much.

"You kept disappearing from the set. I didn't want to miss out on anything, so the last time you left I followed you. First to the van, then I hopped on the back of the van until it drove through a remote-controlled door. A man got out of the van and watched to make sure no one entered with them, so I had to find another way in, which took me a little time. I guess that's when . . . when Linden . . ."

Max's eyes widened as if she were seeing it all over again.

"Come with me," Toby said softly. "And on the way you can tell me what's been going on."

Toby led Max down the stairs and out the secret entrance.

"Where exactly is the Transporter Mark II?" Toby asked as they reached the van.

Max struggled to think. "Ben had it in a leather bag on the floor."

"I need you to distract them while I grab the bag."

There was a look of defeat about Max that Toby had to drive away if his plan was going to work. "Max? Do you understand?"

She looked up slowly and nodded.

"They can't know what has happened, okay?" Max's head bent forward, and she and Toby walked on in silence.

When they arrived at the van some minutes later, Toby shot a worried look at Max before knocking on the door.

Ben saw who it was on the security scanner and leaped up to open the door.

"Max, good to see you. And Toby. Filming finished already?" He looked nervous. So did Eleanor. Max stood there and said nothing.

"Are you okay?" Eleanor asked quietly.

Please, Max, Toby begged under his breath, *please don't lose it*, but just as he thought this, she flung herself into a seat on the other side of the van and filled the small area with wailing howls.

Her uncle and aunt swept over and hugged her. "What is it? What's wrong?"

Toby waited anxiously for what Max would say.

"I'm sorry I was angry and walked out on you before."

Relieved that nothing more had happened, Ben and Eleanor hugged their niece and told her it was okay. Toby caught Max's eye underneath their fussing and hugging. Then he understood. She wasn't losing it, she was doing what he'd asked. His eyes scanned the floor and saw the leather bag. He tucked it into his oversized street-kid clothes and gave her a wink in return. She calmed down and sat up.

"Thanks for being so great. You're the best aunt and uncle anyone could have. Better get back." She hugged them even harder and quickly left the van.

"Bye." Toby waved and ran after Max into the street. "You were great in there."

Max said nothing, and Toby sensed that her crying hadn't simply been a decoy. "Let's get back to the chamber."

After sneaking back in, Toby picked up the discarded packs and handed one to Max. "Are these PFDs hard to operate?"

Max suddenly pulled away. "Why do you keep asking me questions?" she shouted. "Stop bossing me around." She'd never felt so much like giving up in her life. Without Linden, there didn't seem any reason to do anything.

"Max, trust me. I really need your help with this."

Max didn't move. Toby tried again. "How do these work?"

"The lever pulls out and takes you whichever way you move it."

"Sounds easy." He held Max's PFD out to her. She took it reluctantly and put it on. Toby adjusted his PFD and held the Transporter in front of him. Knowing he had no time to be nervous, he followed Max's instructions and entered the destination into the Transporter. "Hold my hand."

Max slowly raised her hand and put it in Toby's.

"Here we go!" he called, and in a few seconds they were being shot like cannonballs through time.

"Aaaaahhhh!"

The tunnel-like whoosh flew past them as they traveled faster than the speed of light, until they stopped and bubbles of reality floated around them. The image of where they were slowly pieced itself together.

"And to think you wanted to keep that from me," Toby breathed. His shirt was torn open and his dark hair danced upright.

Max looked equally disheveled, but after their day as

earthquake victims, it was hard to tell if they really looked that much different. "Where are we?"

"About forty-five minutes ago. Are you sure they can't see us?"

Max nodded as the image of the chamber formed before them. She shivered as she realized she was standing on the balcony with her younger self tied to the rack and Linden below them, facing the last minutes of his life.

"The UN has got a hard enough job trying to bring peace to the world, and you're going to wreck that?"

"Oh, Linden, there you go on your goody-goody crusade again. The UN are a bunch of old fogies dominated by a few countries working for their own benefit. You're smart enough to know that. It's time I benefited as well."

"This Blue's got some issues from childhood I think he needs to work on." Toby adjusted his backpack. "Get your PFD ready."

Max pulled down her lever and watched as her younger self insulted Blue.

"You'll never be half the man my dad is, Blue. You're just a sniveling excuse for a man, who wouldn't know the first thing about loyalty or elegance."

Blue looked up at the younger Max. "I've warned you before about pushing me too far. And now you'll see why. Release him."

Linden was released. He tipped out of the iron cage, struggling to hold on.

"Maybe next time you'll learn when to stay quiet," Blue told the younger Max before leaving the room with his two goons.

Max's stomach became a tangle of guilt and nausea at what was about to happen next, only now, she realized, she wasn't going to let it happen again.

Then Linden fell.

"Let's go!" Max called to Toby. Instead of the usual bumbling and toppling, her PFD took off effortlessly. Toby followed, glad to see the old Max was back, and they both expertly flew their PFDs in tight formation to grab either side of Linden's plummeting body. Their hands partly disappeared into his arms, just like when Max and Linden had visited prehistory, but they kept as firm a hold as they could.

Linden could feel a kind of pressure on his arms but couldn't see anything. All he knew was that his rocketing fall had become a gentle floating to the bottom of the pit.

"I guess this is how guardian angels must feel," said Toby proudly.

Max smiled. Not at Toby's joke but at having Linden back. "Let's get out of here before Blue finds out what's happened. Hold on." They both grabbed Linden's hands as Max took the Transporter Mark II and wrote "Return" on the LCD screen.

"Aaaaahhhh!" all three of them yelled as the whoosh through time took hold.

When they'd landed and the pieces of reality had

formed around them, Linden could see his friends.

"Why do I feel like something weird just happened?"

There was no time for Max to explain. "Beats me," she lied, as she pulled out her palm computer. "We've got to find out where Dad is, return the Transporter to Ben and Eleanor, and finally expose Blue before his plan is complete."

Toby was impressed. "You're pretty scary when you get going."

"You should see her when she really wants to get things done," Linden joked, despite feeling as if he'd just stepped off a high-speed jet.

"Maybe you could both stop talking and just get on with it?" Max raised an eyebrow and tried to look annoyed, but she was secretly overjoyed to have both of them with her in one piece. "Let's go."

CHAPTER 20

A Final Rescue

Using the locator on her palm computer to track down her father, Max led Toby and a still slightly confused Linden down dark, shadowy back lots to a disused section of the film studios.

"The locator says Dad's in this warehouse."

All three looked up at a crumbling building with peeling paint and faded signs. It had no windows, only a single door with a sign that read: DANGER. NO ENTRY.

"Now, that's not very friendly," Toby joked.

Linden held his breath. He knew that Max hated jokes while she was working, but then something weird happened. She laughed.

Toby frowned. He was used to saying things that upset Max, not that made her smile. He could handle the spy stuff—the gadgets, the goons, the bad hair—but Max laughing at one of his jokes freaked him out.

After an awkward silence, they all silently decided to ignore what had happened, and using her laser to break the lock, Max led the way into the warehouse. She and Linden took out their flashlights and walked through the dust-laden air of a cluttered foyer. They passed dead potted plants, torn lounge chairs, and offices with broken blinds and murky windows.

Max had been trying to get the image of Linden's fall out of her head. "Linden?"

"Yeah?" he asked warily, still uneasy about her being furious with him earlier.

Max wanted to apologize for the way she'd behaved, but she wasn't sure how she was going to break it to him that he'd been killed. And the fact that it was her fault.

"Nothing." She sighed.

They walked on with Toby following behind.

"Max?" Linden threw the beam of his flashlight over boxes, crates, and objects hidden by large pieces of material that made them look like giant melted statues. "Are you sure nothing weird happened before? I know this is going to sound strange, but I feel like I'm not in my right body."

She tried to look convincing. "You really have to cut down on the sugar, Linden. It's affecting your thinking."

Linden smiled and instantly Max was filled with an explosive urge to throw her arms around him. Her face filled with a smile that was so wide it started to hurt her cheeks. Linden was back, and she'd never do anything to jeopardize his life again.

"Max?" Linden frowned.

"Mmmm?"

"Why are you staring at me like that?"

"I wasn't staring," Max replied, knowing she had been. She walked on ahead.

Her flashlight lit up ancient-looking camera equipment strung with cobwebs, broken light stands, racks of old clothes, and a large section of tiered seats. There were also some old sets that imitated a palace ballroom, a New York street, a carnival, and a mountain range.

"Is your Danger Meter okay?" Max asked Linden.

"Yep. Yours?"

"Not a whimper." She smiled, happy to be working with him again.

"Where does it say your dad is now?"

Max looked at the locator on her palm computer. "That way." She followed the direction indicated until they reached a tall cement wall.

"Maybe he's on the other side." She took out her heat-sensitive X-ray glasses and examined the wall. "I can see a red glow. It must be him." Her breathing quickened.

"He'll be fine, Max." Linden read her mind before reaching into his bag and taking out one of Plomb's bombs.

Toby looked at the innocent-looking cube. "What's that?"

"It's a dustless, noiseless bomb," Linden explained as he primed it. "It was made by Plomb, the Spy Force bomb expert. Because of his dislike of noise, all his bombs are silent." He stood up and handed the detonator to Max. "The bomb's set."

Max noticed Toby looking at his watch. "What are you doing?"

"Waiting for something."

"Maybe you could concentrate on saving my dad instead," Max suggested, but Toby didn't move. "Well?" Max's hands flew to her hips. Toby gave Linden a nod.

"Happy birthday." They both smiled broadly. Linden

pulled a granola bar from his pocket and stuck a candle in it while Toby lit a match.

"Exactly twelve years ago today the world first heard how well the lungs of Max Remy worked," Toby said importantly.

Max's hands fell slowly from her hips. "How did you know?"

"Your dad," Linden said, as if it were no big deal. "We promised not to say anything. He'd organized a big party for you, but I guess it won't happen now."

Max looked at the mangled granola bar and its crooked candle.

"Well?" Toby said. "Blow it out before the wax ruins it. I'm starving."

Max blew. Linden broke the bar into three pieces, which they shoved quickly into their mouths.

"Dad was going to throw me a party?"

"Yeah," Toby mumbled through an oaty mouthful. "He'd rented an entire amusement park just for us."

Max smiled. So her dad had remembered her birthday after all.

"Stand back," Max commanded. Toby and Linden ran behind a life-size whale, and Max took cover beside a sagging, half-deflated cloud. She held the detonator in her hand. "Three, two, one."

The bomb exploded just as Plomb had said it would. Noiselessly. Toby and Linden raced out to inspect the damage.

"Plomb has made a beauty." Linden admired the collapsed wall before them.

"They really are soundless and dustless." Toby exclaimed, before he realized something was missing. "Max?"

From behind the deflating cloud, which the force of the bomb had burst, Max appeared, covered in a white chalky substance, looking like a ghost in a bad mood. A small dust cloud followed her as she walked past them and climbed through the wrecked wall. Toby and Linden exchanged smirks and followed quietly behind.

"There he is!" Max ran forward and shone her flashlight on a bound and gagged figure lying on the verandah of an old homestead movie set. "Dad?" She knelt beside him as he slowly opened his eyes. He looked tired and disheveled, as if he'd been tied up in this crumpled position for days. Max carefully untied the gag from her father's face.

"Max? Is that you?" he whispered through the darkness.

"Yeah." She wanted to make sure this was her real dad. "Is that you?"

"Ask me something only I would know."

"What is your middle name?"

"Reginald. After my grandfather."

"What food do you hate most in the world?"

"Mushy peas, but I've added jellied eel to that since I saw you last."

It seemed like her dad. At least her old dad, not the angry new one, but after all she knew about Blue she wasn't ready to trust him yet. "What did you say the moment I was born?" she whispered so Toby and Linden wouldn't hear.

He smiled. "I've just seen my first angel."

"Angel?" Toby said way too loudly.

Linden bit his lip and tried not to laugh as Max's head flung around for a death stare. Toby looked away and tried to look innocent. He'd keep, Max thought, as she turned and threw her arms around her father. "It's good to have you back, Dad."

Then he remembered something. "There's this bad guy called Blue who's using the studios to leak secret information to the world."

"Ah, we know," Max admitted as she took out her knife and cut through his ropes.

"You do? Do you also know about the scientist who's here?"

"Fartie?" Linden asked excitedly.

"Yeah. He's over there." Max's dad pointed to a man equally as crumpled as he was, lying in a fake petrol station nearby. Linden ran to see if Fartie was okay.

"We have got to get you both to safety and put an end to Blue's evil plan." Max pulled her palm computer out of her pocket before remembering she needed to be more discreet about being a spy. "I mean, someone else can put an end to Blue's evil plan."

Her dad was curious. "What's that?"

"A computer," she mumbled. "A friend of Ben and Eleanor's gave it to me."

Toby smiled at Max. She was doing a great job of covering, but he had to stop her dad from asking any more questions. "Let me help you up, Mr. Remy."

As he distracted her dad, Max turned away and called Ben and Eleanor. She quickly explained that they'd found her dad and Fartie but avoided saying anything about all the other stuff that had happened: the stolen Matter Transporter, Toby, Linden dying. She knew that when she did tell them, she was going to be in big trouble, but for now her dad was safe and Linden was alive, and that was all she cared about.

CHAPTER 21

A Dressing-Down and a Warning from Spy Force

Ben and Eleanor contacted all the other Spy Force agents on the mission and quickly mobilized the rescue of Max's dad and Dr. Fartie. Apart from a few bruises and dehydration, both men were fine. After hours of questioning by the intelligence agents, Dr. Fartie was escorted to Sleek's Invisible Jet, which transported him back to his home in London. Max's dad was met by an anxious Mee Lin, who had flown in from San Francisco to take him home.

"We'll come too," Max added eagerly, turning to leave the surveillance truck, but Eleanor had other ideas.

"I think it might be better if you stay with us," her aunt suggested in a voice that unnerved Max. "We'll drop you home after your dad's had a chance to rest."

"Is it just me, or is your Danger Meter going crazy too?" Max whispered to Linden.

"There's trouble ahead," Linden confirmed.

"Now tell us what's really been going on," Eleanor demanded slowly.

Linden, Toby, and Max swapped nervous looks. Max swallowed, and then began a complete rundown on everything that had happened since Toby's appearance at the Hollywood restaurant, including how he got there. As much as Max tried, there was no way she could lessen the impact of her story.

"You could have gotten yourselves killed." Ben stomped around the back of the truck when Max's story ended.

"I did." The words were out of Linden's mouth before he could stop them. Ben wasn't amused.

"Lucky for us the Transporter Mark II was able to change that," Ben spelled out. "And what did we tell you about altering the past? We especially warned you about doing that, and you go ahead and do it anyway."

Max had never seen her uncle so angry.

"And, Max, you let a non-agent become part of a Spy Force mission. Secrecy and concealing our identity from non–Spy Force personnel are two of our most important weapons against crime. No offense, Toby."

"It's okay," Toby answered, but even though he was being yelled at, he knew he'd do it all again for a chance to be part of another spy mission.

"And while I remember, you might want to give back the Matter Transporter."

Toby reluctantly took it out of his pocket. Max went to take it, but it was intercepted by Ben.

"We'll talk about a time when you may get this back."

Max drooped in front of her aunt and uncle, sad that she'd messed up so much and even sadder that she'd disappointed them.

Ben had a few more things to say before he was finished, but as much as he tried to stay angry with them, he was also proud of them for completing their mission. He also couldn't imagine life without Linden, and as he thought about how close they'd come to this, his stern look was replaced by a quivering lip. He swooped down and wrapped his bulky arms around all three of them.

As they squirmed in his emotional hold, Toby caught Max's eye and mouthed, "Is he okay?"

Max nodded. Ben was more than okay. He could be a little overemotional at times, but as much as Max hated anything mushy, she wouldn't have him any other way.

"Now." Ben finally pulled himself away, allowing all three to breathe normally again. He wiped his eyes and cheeks with his sleeve. "As we can't have Toby know about Spy Force, we had Sleek bring us the Neuro Memory Atomizer from Quimby's lab."

Eleanor took a small red prism from the many folds of her clothes and explained. "The atomizer rearranges the atoms in the part of the brain that controls memory, enabling Spy Force to erase certain memories without affecting others."

Toby looked wary. "So, that's for me?"

"Don't worry," she said gently. "It'll feel a little strange at first; but after being transported through time, I suspect you'll hardly even notice."

"We're going to transport Toby and erase his memory of the mission at the same time. What's your address so we can get you back home?"

Toby flicked his eyes toward Max, who gave him a nod of encouragement. He rattled off his address, and Ben entered it into the machine. "Right. Time for good-byes."

"Bye, Toby," Linden said. "It was good to hang out with you again."

"No problem." Toby went a bit red. When Toby had first met Linden, he thought he was some dumb kid from the country who dressed out of a secondhand clothing bin. While Linden couldn't be held up as a beacon of fashion, he was a nice guy.

"Can I ask you something?" Max stepped forward.

"Yeah," Toby said warily.

"When you used the Matter Transporter, did you ever have any . . . smelly landings?" She had to know she wasn't the only one the machine dumped on.

"Nope. Every one was like landing in cotton wool."

Max slumped. "Thought so."

When she had first seen Toby in the restaurant she was furious, but now that he was leaving and wasn't going to remember anything, that odd feeling she'd had on the movie set welled inside her again. "See ya," she said, before it got any worse. "And . . . thank you. For everything."

"Yeah. See ya." Toby looked as if he wanted to say more, but didn't.

"I know you're not going to remember this, but next time we meet, try not to break so many rules, okay?" Eleanor smiled and Ben did the customary ruffling of hair.

"See you, kiddo."

Ben programmed the Transporter, and Eleanor held out the Neuro Memory Atomizer, ready to zap the last few days out of Toby's mind forever. When Ben gave the nod, a red beam burst out of the prism, turning Toby translucent pink, with his bones glowing through his skin like a psychedelic X-ray.

"I guess you're not the only one who looks good in pink," Linden said to a transfixed Max. Then just as they were getting used to Toby's new look, he disappeared.

"Will he be okay?" Max asked.

"Apart from a slight headache, he won't feel or remember a thing," Eleanor replied.

"Nothing?" Max seemed disappointed.

"Nothing," Ben answered proudly. "Now, Harrison is waiting for our call."

Harrison? Max thought, her Danger Meter hitting an all-time high. They sat before Eleanor's palm computer as Harrison and Steinberger appeared on the screen.

"Max, Linden. Once again I'm proud to congratulate you on thwarting the evil plans of that smelliest of villains, Mr. Blue." Harrison waved a bandaged hand through the air. "You've done this agency and me barely loud . . . make that 'very proud.'"

Steinberger pressed a button on a small tape recorder that let out a tinny applause. Max and Linden smiled. Steinberger loved these moments.

"And we're glad to hear your father is safe and round . . . ah . . . *sound.*"

"Thanks, Mr. Harrison. What happened to the films?" Max asked.

"With the video from your cameras in the edit room, plus Raychik's statement of what Blue's thugs asked him to do and your dad's account of what happened to him, our agents quickly moved in and put an end to Blue's plan. The films were to be encoded with military secrets of a highly sensitive nature, which had been stolen by some very suspect thieves Blue had made contact with. If they hadn't been stopped, untold makeup would have been inflicted on the world." Harrison's lips scrunched up. "I mean, untold havoc. The encoding devices have been removed and the tampered films recalled."

"So, Raychik wasn't involved?" Max had thought for sure he was working with Blue.

"When he was first approached by Blue, he was told the encoding device would enhance the visual quality of the film, but when he found out what it really did, he refused to cooperate."

"So, why was he at the ski slopes?"

Steinberger answered this one.

"He had a hunch something bad was happening and that whoever was behind it would try to bully your dad into working with them. He didn't know they'd use you to do it."

"Where's Blue now?" Linden asked.

"We're not sure," Harrison said with difficulty. "Unfortunately, he has once again covered his tracks, leaving a man called Albert Power to take the blame—a man who, I'm sure you'll know, doesn't exist."

Max was unnerved by the idea that Blue was still a free man. She'd seen him at his meanest, and if they ran into him again, they might not be so lucky.

"But before I get too carried away,"—Harrison's voice became stern—"we know about the Matter Transporter."

Max felt her Danger Meter slam into her chest.

"You've read the Spy Force manual, Max, so I won't need to tell you that being responsible for the theft of Spy Force equipment is an offense punishable by disqualification from the Force."

Max looked at Linden. Harrison wouldn't really throw her off the Force, would he? Ben tried to give her a hopeful smile, but they all knew that what Harrison said was true. Steinberger stood behind his leader and cast his face downward.

"I'd be very sad to lose you, Max. You certainly are a unique addition to the agency, but rules are there for a season . . . I mean, of course, *reason*."

Linden shuffled. Max couldn't be thrown off the Force. She was his partner and, even though she'd gotten him killed, he didn't want to work with anyone else.

"This Toby should never have been allowed to join you on the mission, for the safety of himself and others." Harrison sighed as if he were about to make a very difficult announcement. "But as he actually helped save Linden's life and complete the mission, I won't take any action . . . this time. And now that Quimby's Neuro Memory Atomizer has been used on him, at least he can't jeopardize the secrecy of Spy Force."

Max let out a relieved sigh. "Thank you, sir. I'll make it up to you next time, I promise. From now on you'll have nothing to worry about."

"Excrement . . . oh, blast, I always get that one mixed up. You know of course that I mean *excellent*. Must go. There are some husky rustlers in Alaska we need to get on to. Well done to you all."

With a beaming smile and a wink from Steinberger, accompanied by marching-band music in the background, Harrison and Steinberger zapped off Eleanor's screen.

CHAPTER 22

A Hard Good-bye

The next few days in LA rocketed by faster than the Transporter Mark II had flung them through time. Max's dad was given time off from the film to recover, and spent every second with Max, Linden, and Mee Lin, and even though her birthday celebration wasn't quite as spectacular as he'd planned, it was the best Max had ever had: just the four of them and Ben and Eleanor over a giant table of Max's favorite food and an afternoon by the pool with no crew, no film set, and no Mr. Blue.

But there was one thing Max needed to know.

"Dad, is it true you and Mee Lin are having a baby?"

Her dad and Mee Lin looked at each other in amazement.

"What makes you ask that?"

She couldn't tell him it was something Blue told her. "I was just wondering."

Her dad grabbed Mee Lin's hand. "We are. We haven't told anybody yet, so I guess that makes you and Linden the first to know."

Max's face fell. How could Blue have known? Her skin tingled at his creepy way of finding out secret information.

Linden looked at Max, hoping she was okay.

"This won't change anything between you and me, Max," her dad explained.

Max realized she must have looked sad. "I know. I mean, that's great news. It'll be excellent to have a little brother or sister."

Her dad opened his arms and smiled. "Come here."

Max disappeared in her dad's hug as Ben and Eleanor swooped in and offered their mushy congratulations.

Even though they'd traveled back in time and then forward again, Max never understood why all the good times in her life went so fast. It seemed as if they'd only just arrived, but when she looked up again, they were standing at the airport surrounded by bags and tourists and annoying announcements. Max had said a lot of good-byes in her life but this was the hardest. Mee Lin hugged her and told her how happy she was to have met her, before handing her a parcel.

"Thanks," Max managed, wondering what kind of pink creation was inside the wrapping. "I'm glad I met you, too."

Ben and Eleanor looked as if they weren't going to let Max's dad go, until they heard the final call for their plane. A huge gulp of air swept into Max's lungs as she knew this was it. She did all she could not to cry. "Bye, Dad."

"Bye, muffin." Before she knew what had happened, Max was being shuffled through security doors and along passages, and was on the plane heading back home.

"Are you going to open that?" Linden pointed to Mee Lin's parcel in Max's lap.

"I would, but I've had enough pink for this trip."

"Come on, you can handle a little more," Linden sputtered through a packet of pretzels.

226

Max reluctantly tore open the wrapping and was relieved to find an orange T-shirt with the words, "Movie Director, LA."

"I guess she got the pink thing, after all." Linden smiled before adding, "Your dad's really nice."

"Yeah, he is."

"I'm sorry that I thought he might have been involved with Blue. It's just that . . ."

"That's okay." Max smiled and added because she could, "It's good for you to be wrong sometimes."

"Maybe all that traveling through time made my head a bit fuzzy." He fluffed up his wild hair.

Max laughed. "We did it, though. We completed another mission."

"Yeah. We did. Even if you did get me killed."

Max never wanted to think about that again.

"I'm sorry, Linden. Eleanor once told me when you find a great partner, you have to remember that you have something special." She blushed uncontrollably, then she said decisively, "From now on I'm not going to lose my temper, and no matter how angry I get I'll always think before I speak."

Just at that moment a steward carrying a tray tripped and sent ice-cold drinks cascading into Max's lap. "Hey, mud brain. Why don't you look where you're going? Is it that hard to—" Max stopped as she caught Linden's look.

The steward gave her a cloth to wipe herself down. "I'm so sorry," he said.

Max smiled as sweetly as she could. "That's okay," she said proudly. After a few more apologies the guy walked off and Max turned to Linden.

"Maybe it'll take a little time," he said.

She smiled. It was good to have Linden with her again, and from now on she'd do everything to be the best partner she could be.

One final weird thing . . .

On Max's first day back at school she flinched when she saw Toby and his group heading toward her. She looked at his face, trying to work out if he was going to be his usual revolting self or whether he would say something nice.

Toby stopped in front of her, but Max got in first. "I see you've brought your little group of primate friends. Must go through a lot of antiseptic having to drag their knuckles on the ground."

Toby's friends sniggered and pretended to be offended, but they knew Toby would have something clever lined up for her. The sniggering soon stopped, followed by an awkward silence as he said nothing.

Max gave it another shot. "What's wrong? Did your brain finally decide to move into a better-looking head?"

One of Toby's friends started laughing, until the stares

of the others quickly cut him off. This was getting embarrassing. Toby never took mouthing from anyone. Especially Max. His friends stood by wondering why he was doing nothing.

Toby frowned. He wasn't sure himself what was happening. He wanted to say something cutting, but all he came out with was, "Hi, Max."

There was a strange pause like when people know something bad has happened but don't know what to do about it.

Toby walked away with his friends following, wanting an explanation.

"Don't say anything," Toby ordered. "I feel weird enough as it is."

Max smiled. Even though the Neuro Memory Atomizer had been used on Toby, maybe there were still parts of their Hollywood mission he couldn't let go of, like the part where he'd realized he liked Max. And what about the part where Max had realized she liked Toby?

Suddenly she didn't feel well. As the bell chimed throughout the school grounds, Max picked up her bag and headed to class, eager to have something other than Toby and churning stomachs to think about.